SCHOOL FOR SAUCY SORCERESSES

MISTY'S MAGICK & MAYHEM: BOOK 2

Carolina Mac & Auburn Tempest

To: Those who draw strength from the moon.

You had the power all along, my dear.
—GLINDA, THE GOOD WITCH

CHAPTER ONE

Wednesday, February 1st.

Nine Saint Gillian Street. New Orleans

The LeJeune Book of Shadows lay open to page ninety-nine on the long black worktable. Although the edges of the parchment pages were ragged and torn on some of the more frequently used spells, for the age of the book, it was in remarkably fine condition.

Surrounded by tools of the trade, and jars of ingredients used by those who knew the ways of the powerful ones who had gone before, the LeJeune Book of Shadows had a history and was coveted and sought by many of those who knew of its existence.

Protecting the family tome and her magickal heritage was Mystere LeJeune's destiny and her duty. A rocky road and a dangerous one to follow, she was born to it. Committed to her calling since the day of her birth, and nothing and no one could make her waver.

The list of ingredients on page ninety-nine had been tested for their purity and carefully measured and added to the cauldron bubbling on the big black stove.

"It smells wonderful, Mother, but do you think we'll

need that much?"

Claire LeJeune painted a beautiful picture as she stood, stirring the pot with an oversized wooden ladle. A well-rounded witch and gifted psychic in her mid-fifties, Claire stood tall and straight as a reed, her long dark hair glistening in the morning sun. "If his niece is as much trouble as Luke says she is, we might need a lot more."

"What time will Luke be back from Baton Rouge with her?" asked Casey. He sipped coffee at the far side of the table wearing his reflector shades, his Saint's cap hiding most of his long dark hair.

The kitchen was bright in the morning while the sun loitered in the eastern sky. During Misty's recent renovations, she'd ripped the old lace curtains down and hadn't replaced them. Even the dark red walls and the ceiling rafters hung with hundreds of bundles of dried herbs and flowers did little to dull the brilliance.

"Baton Rouge isn't far," said Misty. "If the traffic is light, Luke should be back by noon."

"I should have gone with him," said Luke's grandmother. "I had a good relationship with Rowanne when she was a girl."

"The trip might have been tiring for you, Gran," said Misty. "I'm sure Luke can manage one sixteen-year-old."

Casey crossed the kitchen to refill his coffee mug and turned to Claire. "Are we starting our second semester today, Madam Claire, or waiting until Rowanne gets settled in?"

Casey Nichols, a handsome dark-haired seventeen-year-old, was the ward of Misty's ex-boyfriend, Blaine Blackmore. The boy had moved temporarily to New Orleans to study magick and was quickly becoming a skilled witch under the tutelage of Claire and Misty LeJeune.

Misty's mom smiled. "I think you and I will go up and give the classroom a good cleansing, Casey, and we'll get ready to begin. I've printed out a tentative curriculum of what y'all need to learn, and we have a lot to cover this semester."

"Happy to help, Madam."

Luke returned with his niece at five minutes to twelve, as Misty predicted. Angelique was in the process of setting the table.

"We're just in time for lunch, Rowanne," said Luke with a smile. "That's lucky."

"Not hungry," she said, her face screwed in a snarl. "I'm not going to eat, and I'm not staying here in this creepy house no matter what my dad says."

Small for sixteen, Rowanne Hyslop, at just over five feet tall, reminded Luke of a Hallowe'en firecracker. A pretty face obscured with overdone Goth makeup, a ring in her nose, and all topped off with spiky red hair.

Misty smiled sweetly, as Luke made the introductions. "Rowanne, this is Misty."

"Aw, the beautiful and all-powerful Madam LeJeune. Our family has power, too, you know. I got power from my great-gran, and I know how to use it. Where is she?"

"Don't be rude to Misty," snapped Luke. "Gran is in the dining room. Why don't you go in and say hello to her?"

Rowanne gave Luke the stink-eye, then stomped into the next room, her knee-high army boots clunking on the hardwood, the laces dragging along behind.

Luke sighed and pulled Misty into a hug. "She's a lot to cope with, sweetheart. I still don't think this is a good idea."

"We have the room," said Misty, "and Mother has a way with young people. She might be able to turn her around. Casey and the girls might be a good influence on her, too."

Luke was skeptical. "She was expelled from her high school for hexing the other students."

"Did her spells work?" asked Misty.

Luke chuckled. "No. I don't think so."

"I was expelled once, wasn't I, Daddy?" Misty smiled and looked to the corner of the kitchen—Josiah LeJeune's favorite spot to haunt. A moment later, she giggled and continued. "He was called into the principal's office and given a harsh lecture on his wild and unruly daughter. He had to pay thirty dollars for the damages the day I got furious over something and blew out all the light bulbs in the lunchroom."

Luke chuckled. "Shit happens."

After lunch, Misty took Rowanne upstairs to the second floor to show her the room she'd made ready for her next to her great-grandmother's room. Luke had already carried her luggage upstairs and placed it on her bed.

"This place is a dump," Rowanne huffed. "It's old and stuffy and dark... and it smells like musty assholes."

"What a rude and indignant guest," said Josiah. Of course, Rowanne couldn't hear him. Only Misty and Claire could hear him, and sometimes Luke or Angelique.

Misty ignored Rowanne. She reached out her hand and pointed towards the candle on the dresser, and with a little *poof*, it burst into flame.

Rowanne's feigned indifference, but Misty caught the widening of her eyes as she picked up her backpack. "I think I'll work on my laptop for a while."

"You can do that later," she said. "Mother and the other students are waiting for you upstairs."

"I'm not going up there. I want to be alone for a while."

"Your loss." Misty left her in her room, closed the door, and went back downstairs. "She wants to stay in her room, she hates her room, and refused to go upstairs to class and be with the others."

Luke sighed, the tension of the day getting to him. "I'll see what I can do." He plodded up the stairs and tapped twice on his niece's door. "Rowanne, can I come in?"

"No. I told that woman that I want to be by myself for a while. Can I get some damned privacy?"

"I'll give you an hour," Luke said through the door, "then I'll be back to take you up to the classroom and introduce you to the other students."

"Yeah, whatever."

Misty met him in the hallway. "Any luck?"

"She just got here, and she's upset. Let her be for an hour, and then I'll take her up and introduce her."

"Your call, sweet thing." Misty kissed him and pressed him up against the wall.

"I have an idea," Luke whispered. "Let's stay in our room for an hour and not think about family troubles."

Misty glanced at the grandfather clock standing sentinel in the upstairs hallway. "I have a client in three minutes."

Luke groaned.

Angelique lit the candles in the front parlor in readiness for Misty's first client of the day. Leo Pinoit was a regular and had been for several years. He'd been absent for a while, and Misty was looking forward to catching up. The last time he'd been to the house for a reading was New Year's Day.

Misty greeted him in the foyer and immediately knew that something was off. Thin and pale, Leo was far from his robust overfed self of only one month ago. Writing a *Best Places to Eat in the Big Easy* column had elevated Leo to celebrity status in the city and also kept him slightly above his ideal weight.

Misty took his coat and hung it in the closet. "Lovely to see you, Leo. Have you been ill?"

"Did you discern that with your powers, Madam

LeJeune? Or do I look like crap?"

Misty took his hand and led him into the parlor. "Perhaps a little of both. Sit, Angelique will get you some restorative tea."

Leo cast Angelique an affectionate smile. "I would love the one you make with the ground herbs and cinnamon if you have the ingredients."

"Right away, sir." Angelique hurried off to the kitchen.

Misty shuffled the cards a couple of times then passed them to Leo to shuffle. "Tell me what's happened."

As he mixed the deck, he said, "A printed invitation came in the mail and invited me to an opening in the quarter. I receive invitations to so many all over the city, and in Baton Rouge, I can only attend a limited number. A person can only eat so many gourmet meals in a week." He smiled weakly, and Misty noticed the hollows in his cheeks.

"I accepted by telephone, and my assistant put the date in my planner. The night of the opening, Craig and I arrived and were welcomed by the owner. He showed us to a lavishly set table, and I must admit, the décor was to die for."

Angelique brought Leo his tea and smiled at him. He patted her hand and continued. "The owner donned an apron and served me himself. Somewhat unusual, but not unheard of, so I paid little attention to the oddity of it."

"Wasn't the place packed on opening night?" asked Misty.

"That should have been my first clue," said Leo. "When I arrived, and the restaurant was empty, I was taken aback, but the owner—a man named Marvin Downes—said it was the pre-opening, by invitation only, and other special guests would come later."

"Was the food good? What's their specialty?"

"Italian, mixed with local, and that's one of the reasons I went. My followers depend on me to sort out the best from the mundane when there are so many establishments serving the same menu."

Misty nodded. "And something untoward happened?"

"Untoward? Yes, definitely. The marinara sauce was poisoned. Marvin Downes tried to kill me."

"Kill you? Why would he?"

"Craig did some digging. As it turned out, Mr. Downes had another restaurant some years ago. After I reviewed it unfavorably in the magazine, he went out of business."

Misty frowned. "If he served poor quality food the first time around, you didn't put him out of business. He can't hold you accountable for his shortcomings."

"True enough. I've given hundreds of mediocre reviews in my career, and no one tried to knock me off. "They may have been angry. They may have even thought about getting back at me, but no one ever poisoned me."

"Did you go to the police?"

"Craig insisted that I inform the police when I got out of the hospital, but it was too late for any proof to be obtained. I was in intensive care for several days before they were certain I would live."

"Oh, my goodness," said Misty. "I'm going to tell Luke this story and see what he thinks."

"There's nothing he can do, dear, so long after the fact. But thank you for the thought."

"The least he can do is check on the status of your investigation, Leo. Would you mind if he did that?"

"Not at all. Craig called NOPD several times, but each time they told him they had no new leads."

Luke gave Rowanne a reasonable amount of time alone in her room to get herself settled and then knocked on the door and tried again. "Rowanne, it's me, Uncle Luke. Come out of there, honey. I want to take you upstairs and introduce you to the other students."

"Go away, Uncle Luke. I'm not going to be a student at this crazy fake witch school."

Luke opened the door wide and stood there in the doorway, glaring at Rowanne, sprawled on her bed. "Wrong. You *are* going up to meet the others, and you're going to do it right now. I'm not putting up with this."

Rowanne laughed. "What will you do to me? What can you do? Nothing. That's what you'll do."

Luke pulled his wand out of the pocket of his jeans and pointed it at Rowanne.

Her eyes widened, and she jumped off the bed. "Okay, I'm getting up. Don't zap me, Uncle Luke."

Luke smiled. "Better. You'll have fun with the other

kids."

"No, I won't."

Luke marched Rowanne up the narrow staircase to the third floor and blocked her escape while he introduced her to the others. "Rowanne, you already met Casey at lunch. And these lovely ladies are Diana, sitting next to Casey, then Michele beside Diana and Charlotte at the end of the table."

"You can sit here, dear," said Claire, pointing to the empty chair they'd added. "Diana got you a notebook and pen from the supply cupboard."

"I'm not taking notes."

"Well, that's up to you," said Claire. "Perhaps you're an auditory learner. We all retain information in different ways."

"You can't teach me anything I don't already know. I'm gifted in the dark arts."

"Wonderful," said Claire. "Perhaps you'll be inspired to share a tiny portion of your knowledge with us when you get to know us better."

"Don't think so."

Casey nodded his head, and Rowanne swiveled around to face him. "What are you staring at, witch boy?"

"A witch bitch, that's what."

"*Enough.*" Luke raised his voice, a rare occurrence indeed. "All of you listen to Madam LeJeune and try to learn something useful. That's why y'all are here."

"Thank you, Luke." Claire smiled. "Shall we continue?"

***

Claire waited while Luke retreated to the second floor, and then gathered the attention of her students. "This morning, we're going to talk about conjuring. Counting on the power of a group effort when casting a circle is one thing, but each of you must be able to do each step alone, and I hope you've practiced. Who's been practicing everything we learned in semester one?"

The original four put up their hands.

Rowanne huffed.

"Have you something to say, dear?"

"I don't need to practice. I'm a hereditary witch. My power comes from my great-grandmother, my grandmother, and my father. Our family has generations of magick to call upon."

"And powers can slip away and become unruly if you don't constantly practice," said Claire. "If you're imbibed with so much magick, let us see your skill with a wand, young lady."

Rowanne smiled as she pulled a black wand decorated with skulls out of her pocket. She pointed her wand at the window and hollered out a spell. "Watch this."

> *King of night*
> *Hide morning light*
> *Through windowpane*
> *Let me see rain*
> *So mote it be.*

The girls rushed to the window and looked up into the

sky to see if it was clouding over. The mid-afternoon sun continued to shine brightly.

Rowanne hollered out the spell again, and when nothing happened, she grabbed her wand with both hands and snapped it in two. "This wand is no fucking good."

"Enough, young lady," said Claire. "I don't want to hear a word out of you until the end of the day."

"Ha ha," shrieked Rowanne, "like you can make me keep quiet if I don't want to be quiet?"

Without bothering to use her wand, Claire pointed a finger at the girl.

So much to say
Words run like a river
Lips become sealed
With a sneeze and a shiver

Ah-choo. Rowanne sneezed, then shuddered. Her dark brown eyes widened as she sat still as a statue and didn't say a word.

Casey smiled. "Can we get on with the lesson now?"

Upset by his niece's behavior, Luke plodded downstairs thinking he and Misty had made a grave mistake telling his brother they'd take over parenting duties for a while to give him a break. Recovering from heart surgery, Luke's brother didn't need the stress of a teenage witch rebelling daily under his roof.

He wandered into the front parlor as Misty was

putting the Tarot cards away.

"Just in time, sweetheart," said Misty. "Leo needs to talk to you about something important."

Luke shook hands with Leo. "I've read your column from time to time, sir, and often taken your advice on where to eat in the city of unlimited food choices."

"Thank you," said Leo. "And I don't think I'll bother you with my problem. It's in the past, and I'm over it."

Luke sat down at the table. "Go ahead and tell me, sir. I need a diversion today. A big one."

Leo told Luke a tale of poison and revenge, and before he'd gone too far, Luke had his notebook out writing down what he deemed to be important. "I can see it would have been much too late to take a sample of the food you ate. If the attempt was deliberate, that's the first thing the would-be-killer would do is destroy the evidence."

Leo nodded. "It is pointless to hash this all up now."

"And since the poisoning, have you written anything in the magazine about Mr. Downe's new restaurant?"

Leo shook his head. "No. It seems, when it comes to a choice between my life and my craft, I'm a bit of a coward."

"You had a scare. Maybe that's what Mr. Downe intended, and maybe it wasn't. It won't hurt to dig into his background a little and see if he has anything lurking that he'd rather keep hidden from the public."

"I appreciate your taking the time, sir," said Leo, "and as I've offered Madam LeJeune time and again, I would love to have you both as my guests at an establishment of your choice."

Luke enjoyed seeing Misty's smile. She obviously liked and respected Leo and had mentioned before that she'd like to experience a meal with him and live for an evening in his shoes. "We'd love to do that, wouldn't we sweetheart? We haven't been out together in a while."

Leo stood up and prepared to leave. "I'll make reservations and call. I'm so pleased to have you accept my invitation."

Misty opened the closet and held Leo's coat for him. "Take care of yourself, Leo. I'm looking forward to our dinner."

After Leo left, Luke stood at the bottom of the staircase and listened. "It sounds quiet up there. Do you think that's a good sign or bad?"

Misty giggled. "Definitely bad. Let's go up."

Luke and Misty reached the third floor and peeked in at Claire and the students. Casey, Michele, Diana, and Charlotte were taking turns calling the corners, and Rowanne was sitting silent at the end of the table watching them. She wasn't uttering a single word.

Misty smiled.

Mother is working her magick.

CHAPTER TWO

Thursday, February 2nd.

<u>Nine Saint Gillian Street. New Orleans</u>

Luke stared at the empty seat at the breakfast table, annoyed that Rowanne hadn't been polite enough to join them.

"It's all right," said Misty. "Give her time to adjust."

"No, Mist, it's not all right. It's rude, and one thing I'm not putting up with is rude behavior from a sixteen-year-old girl."

"Do you want me to go up and get her?" asked Casey.

Luke set his fork down beside his half-finished plate of ham and eggs and sighed. "No, I'll go."

He trudged up the mahogany staircase, walked down the long hallway and tapped on her door. "Rowanne, breakfast. Are you coming down?"

"Nope. Not hungry. Not getting up yet."

"You better get up soon. The class starts at nine."

"Not going to the stupid class."

Luke tried the door, and it was locked. "You are going to class, Rowanne, and you should eat breakfast beforehand."

"You can't make me eat," she called out, "and you can't make me learn if I don't want to."

Luke blew out a breath and wondered if he'd made a colossal mistake bringing his niece to New Orleans. He'd do anything to help his brother, but... Luke closed his eyes and asked the goddess to aid in his brother, Sam's recovery.

Blessed be.

At eight forty-five, Charlotte, Diana, and Michele arrived for school. Hoodoo barked and bounced in the front foyer as they shed their jackets and hung them in the closet. Each of them patted Hoodoo's head and said hello to the big Bernese.

"I'm so excited for this semester," said Charlotte, her blue eyes magnified behind the lenses of her dark-rimmed glasses. Her dark hair hung loosely around her shoulders. "I've been practicing at home in our apartment, and I'm gaining more control of my powers. I'm making progress. I can feel it."

Claire smiled at her. "The harder you work, the more successful you will be. When Josiah was alive, he spent hours with Mystere, making her practice."

"And look at her today," said Diana, "the most powerful witch in New Orleans." Diana was the smallest and youngest of the three. She was a slight, young thing, with olive skin and spiky black hair.

A voice came from the top of the staircase, and the

girls turned and looked up. "Misty won't be the most powerful for much longer," hollered Rowanne. "I'll be taking over top spot."

"Then get up to the classroom and prove it," Casey hollered back at her. "You brag a lot, Rowanne, but you haven't shown us a damned thing."

Claire smiled as she heard Rowanne clumping up to the attic in her army boots. "Good job, Casey," she whispered.

Casey wasn't wearing his happy face.

Luke poured his second cup of coffee and sat in the kitchen while Misty and Angelique worked on one of the orders that had come in online. "I'm going to Marvin Downe's restaurant for lunch, sweetheart. Would you consider joining me on a little fishing trip?"

"Ooh," said Misty. "I would so love that. He should pay for trying to kill Leo."

"We can't say he did anything to Leo until we have evidence," said Luke. "That's the way it works."

"Then we'll have to get the evidence, won't we?"

Luke smiled. "We can try. Until we leave, I'll be at my desk probing into dark deeds Mr. Downe has done in the past."

Misty turned to the corner of the kitchen. "Daddy's saying he used to follow Leo's column and take Mother to the restaurants Leo raved about."

"And were they worth the raves, Josiah?" Luke asked.

Misty nodded. "All but one were wonderful."

"Which one wasn't?"

Misty stared off into that corner with nothing but love in her beautiful green gaze. "Daddy says he can't remember which one didn't measure up to Leo's review, but Mother will. We should ask her."

"Thank you, sir. We'll do that."

Claire began the morning session with a discussion on the correct procedure for casting a circle. "Everyone in this room should have cast a personal circle by now."

"Nothing to it," said Rowanne fiddling with the broken pieces of her wand still lying on the table. "I can cast y'all one right now."

"No, thanks, dear," said Claire. "We must never cast a circle while angry. No harmony can come from it."

"I've never had trouble with any of my circles," said Rowanne. "They always work perfectly."

"Uh-huh," said Claire. "To achieve a high level of power, dear, you must first remove all your negativity."

"I'm not negative," snarled Rowanne. "You don't know me, Madam, and you certainly don't know what I'm capable of. Nobody does."

Claire continued without addressing the girl's tantrum. "Casey, why don't you light a smudge and we'll cleanse the room before we start. While Casey does that, let's all enjoy a refreshing drink of harmonious nectar."

At the sideboard, Claire poured everyone a glass of the red concoction she'd prepared and refrigerated in quart sealers. Charlotte hopped up and passed out the glasses.

"This is yummy, Madam," said Diana. "I love it."

"Enjoy. I made a large batch."

Claire watched Rowanne carefully as she took one sip of the potion to test it. After tasting it, she tipped up the glass and drank it down.

Now we can get down to business.

Downe's Italian Eatery, New Orleans

The hostess showed Misty and Luke to a table next to the wall. Every table was decked out with all the conventional trappings of an Italian restaurant: red and white checkered tablecloths and a candle in a Chianti fiasco.

Why did Leo say the décor was to die for?

They sat down, and the hostess placed menus in front of them. She smiled and pointed at the blackboard on the wall. "The lunch specials are listed on the board. Your server is Karen, and she'll be right with you."

"So far so good," said Luke. "Seems to be business as usual to me."

Misty glanced around at all the posters on the walls. "The place seems a little cliché to me, Lukey. He could have leveled up a notch or two."

"Maybe this is the look customers expect. He could have had a decorator."

Misty giggled. "No way."

Luke handed her the wine list. "Pick something you

like, sweetheart. I'll have a beer."

When their server introduced herself, Misty ordered a glass of the house red, and Luke asked for Miller draft.

"I'll wander to the ladies' room and see if I pick anything up," said Misty. "Save my spot."

"Your spot will always be next to me, sweetheart."

Misty pulled back Luke's long auburn hair and kissed his neck. "Good answer."

When their server brought the drinks, Luke asked, "Is Mr. Downe here today?"

"Not yet, sir. He usually arrives to prepare for the dinner hour. Sometimes he likes to cook the main entrée himself. He is a chef."

"Oh, I didn't realize," said Luke. He took a long pull on his beer. "Chef. Uh-huh."

Misty left the ladies' room and ventured farther down the hallway to where two doors were marked private. Covering the knob with the tail of her flowery top, she gave it a turn, and it didn't budge. Locked.

She moved to the next door and did the same thing. The door opened without a sound. She stepped in, picked up a pen from the desk and shoved it into her pocket, then retreated into the hall and closed the door.

Her wine awaited her when she returned to the table.

Luke raised an eyebrow. "You were gone a while. I was beginning to worry."

"I stole a pen for later."

Luke grinned. "Petty theft. Shall I arrest you for that?"

Misty giggled. "If you want me handcuffed, all you have to do is ask, sugar."

Luke barked out a laugh and sobered as the server returned to take their order. Misty hadn't had a chance to check out the menu, so gestured for Luke to go first.

"I'll have the chicken fettuccini special, with the salad, not soup," Luke said.

Misty nodded and handed back her menu. "Sure. I'll have the same."

Nine Saint Gillian Street

After their lunch break, Casey took Hoo with him and stepped out onto the back porch for a smoke. He was watching the dog circling the yard slowly and carefully, not yet recovered from being poisoned by the Castille family. The vet said after days of not eating, it would take the big Bernese a while to regain his strength.

The door opened behind him, and Rowanne came out with a pack of Tijuana Smalls in her hand. Casey tried not to laugh out loud. Instead, he asked her if she needed a light.

"Yeah, thanks if you have one handy."

Casey flicked his lighter and held it to the end of her smoke.

After a lengthy coughing fit, Rowanne was able to speak. "Haven't smoked in a few days. My prick of a father wouldn't let me smoke at our house."

Casey nodded. He wasn't wasting conversation on a mean piece of work like her. He lived on the street as a runaway. He knew how good they had it having Misty and Luke watching out for them. He finished his cigarette, left her on the porch, and went back inside.

The afternoon lesson on closing the cast circle had already started when Rowanne came clumping up the attic stairs.

"I figured y'all wouldn't wait for me," she aimed her remark at Claire.

Claire smiled. This girl had so much anger bottled up inside her it was a wonder she didn't explode. "Sit down, dear, and tell me exactly how you would close a circle."

"I would do it in the reverse order from the casting we did this morning."

"Good. Now verbalize the steps for me."

Rowanne turned and curled her lip at Casey. "Let him do it. He thinks he knows how to do everything."

Claire raised a brow. "Casey is a competent witch. He works hard, he listens, and he learns. You would do well to learn from him."

"I don't listen to people, I don't like."

Casey chuckled and raised his palms. "Then please don't like me because I wouldn't want you to do me any favors."

Diana hopped up and turned on the kettle. "Who's for tea?"

"Lovely, Diana," Claire said, addressing the group. "When we're finished our lesson this afternoon, Diana has agreed to give each of us a tea leaf reading. Tasseography is an age-old practice of divination. Diana's grandmother is skilled in the art and passed along her knowledge to Diana."

Rowanne scoffed. "I'm not drinking tea. Tea is for old people."

"That's fine, Rowanne. No one will make you drink tea, dear. Why don't you have some more of the punch I made."

"Actually, I don't mind that stuff." She clumped over to the sideboard and refilled her glass.

Claire smiled, watching her.

Luke was parking Misty's big, black truck in the lane behind her property when Misty's cell rang. "Leo, nice of you to call... Uh-huh, Clancy's for tomorrow night at eight... Yes, thank you. Oh, yes, I love Clancy's. I'm so looking forward to seeing you and Craig."

Luke grinned as he locked up the truck. "Can't believe he got us into Clancy's on such short notice."

"Leo has clout with the restauranteurs in the city. Mmm..." said Misty. "I can taste the crab cakes now."

Misty hung her cape in the front hall closet, then floated up to the third floor to see if her mother needed help with the afternoon lesson.

"Hope I'm not interrupting. Anything I can help with?"

"I don't think so, dear, but you're welcome to join us.

We love having you here."

Diana gestured to the teapot on the sideboard. "I made loose tea so I could give everyone a reading."

"Oh, what fun," said Misty. "Not one of my skills at all, I'm afraid, but I'd love to watch y'all."

Diana hopped up and poured everybody except Rowanne, a cup of tea in a china cup with a saucer.

"Isn't Rowanne joining in for tea?" asked Misty.

Rowanne shook head, her red hair whipping around her shoulders. "Nope. Like I told them. I hate tea, and I'm not an old lady."

"Too bad you'll miss out on the fun."

Rowanne screwed up her face and scowled at her. "You're kidding, right? If you think tea is fun, something's seriously wrong with you."

"Spells are my kind of fun, young lady." Misty pointed her finger at Rowanne and chanted.

> *Unkind words no longer spoken*
> *Evermore the spell unbroken*
> *Smile while searching for life's token*
> *Leave all other's faults unspoken*
> *So mote it be.*

Rowanne smirked. "Your dumb spell won't work on me. I can reverse anything you send my way."

"Then reverse away, Rowanne. In the meantime, would you care for some tea?"

Rowanne smiled. "Yes, please. I'd love some."

Diana giggled and poured another cup.

After dinner was over and Rowanne had gone to her room to talk to her Facebook friends, Misty and Luke retired to the sitting room to see if the pen taken from Marvin Downe's office earlier in the day had any secrets to reveal.

In case Misty felt faint like she sometimes did after going into a deep trance, Luke brought in a cup of tea and a little plate of freshly-baked sweets for her. He pulled out his notebook and pen and winked at her. "Whenever you're ready, sweetheart."

Casey walked in and sat down. "Can I watch?"

"Sure," said Misty. "Might be nothing."

Misty picked up the pen, closed her eyes, and held it tightly in both her hands. She was silent for several minutes before she spoke. "Dark intentions fill him. Anger and revenge color his every thought. He thinks of nothing else. It's an obsession."

Luke wrote down every word. Quiet until Misty opened her eyes. "Anything interesting?"

"Not much. I think the pen was too small. I need something more substantial."

"Like...?"

"Clothing, a piece of his jewelry—a watch."

"I don't know how we would obtain any of those things," said Luke. "Short of committing B&E into his residence and robbing the man."

Rowanne's phone alarm went off right on time at three a.m., and she wasted no time getting out of bed. She'd slept in her clothes and packed up all her belongings the night before, so there was little to do, but pick up her suitcase and her backpack and tiptoe down the stairs to the front door.

She knew the security alarm code. Uncle Luke changed it every couple of days, but he'd made sure she knew what it was. Big mistake. She disarmed the thing, opened the door a crack, slipped out, and closed the door softly behind her.

The cold, crisp night air woke her right up, and she felt good. She was free.

As she stepped through the squeaky front gate onto the sidewalk, she mumbled a sarcastic goodbye. "Thanks for nothing, Uncle Luke, and your super witch girlfriend."

She needed freedom to become the witch she wanted to be. There was nothing these goodie-two-shoe witches could teach her that she didn't already know.

She walked for an hour towards the bus terminal. It had seemed so much closer on the Google map she printed out.

At the next corner, she plopped down in a bus shelter to rest her legs and take another look at the map. She pulled it out of her backpack, and while she studied it, she lit up a smoke.

A couple of older kids in leather jackets ran into the shelter and sat down next to her. "Where you going, sweetheart?"

"None of your business." She studied their long hair, tattoos, and ragged jeans and sneered at them. "What are you, gangers?"

The boys laughed.

"Feisty. That's the way we like them," said one.

"You should come with us."

Rowanne laughed. "Yeah, I don't think so."

"Okay, how about, you're *coming* with us." The guy beside her grabbed her arm and tried to pull her to her feet.

She booted him in the shin with her army boot. "Think again, asshole. I'm not going anywhere with the likes of y'all."

"Wrong, little red."

The sting on her neck bit her skin an instant before everything went black.

CHAPTER THREE

Friday, February 3rd.

<u>Nine Saint Gillian Street. New Orleans</u>

Luke finished with his first smoke of the day and headed in from the backyard to the kitchen. Angelique was up at the crack of dawn, baking a huge pan of cornbread for breakfast. The aroma had wafted out of the oven and floated up the stairs enticing him as the first customer to the kitchen.

Angelique lived her whole life and raised two sons in the bayou west of Houma. A large woman with dark complexion and waist-length ebony hair, Angelique had a charming face and a disposition to match.

She spoke Cajun French complicated with a local dialect making her difficult to understand. He and Misty had little trouble, but he'd been raised in the bayou too, so there was that.

A hoodoo practitioner specializing in doll magick, and a skilled jewelry maker, she made the perfect assistant for Misty.

She greeted him with a hot cup of coffee and a smile when he came inside. The February wind whipping off the waters of the Gulf sent nippy air into the city, and Luke knew better than to go out without a jacket. With his thick coat of fur, Hoodoo didn't mind the cold, but Luke shivered and was thankful for the coffee.

"Gran," he said when his grandmother shuffled into the kitchen fully dressed. "Gran, why are you up so early?"

"I dreamed Rowanne ran away and couldn't get back to sleep. I got up and looked in her room, and it's true, Lukey. She's gone."

"She ran away?" Luke's heartbeat double-timed as he ran upstairs to check. Fighting off the panic overtaking him, he opened the door of Rowanne's room and glanced around. The bed was messed up, and all her clothes were gone. He checked the desk, and her laptop was gone too.

"Yep. Gone."

He phoned his brother in Baton Rouge and left a message. "Sam, sorry to lay this on you, but Rowanne has taken off. Keep an eye out for her, would you? She might head home. I'm looking for her here. Try not to worry."

He's got a bad heart, Rowanne. Don't be a little shit.

Luke ran into Casey in the upstairs hall. "I heard you leaving a message. Is she gone?"

"I didn't hear her in the night, did you?" asked Luke.

"Nope, but we have a house full of psychics, so we should be able to get a read on where she is."

"Let's do that at breakfast," said Luke. "Super idea."

"Just a thought... but if she opened the door in the middle of the night, wouldn't the alarm have gone off?"

"Should have. Let me check." Luke booked it down the stairs and slid to a stop in front of the panel, two feet from the door. "The system is turned off."

"Did she know how to do it?" asked Casey.

"Yep, cause like a dummy, I showed her."

After everyone had eaten and had a fresh cup of caffeine, Misty sat with her mother, Luke, his Grandmother, Angelique, and Casey. They held hands around the long table and focused their combined concentration on the whereabouts of Rowanne.

Sitting in total silence with a white candle burning in the center of their circle, they waited for information to come to their minds from a different plane.

When Josiah spoke from his spot in the corner of the kitchen, the silence was broken. Misty jumped.

"She headed for the bus terminal to go back home, but she never made it that far."

"Why not, Daddy? What stopped her?"

"A couple of guys scooped her, and she's being held in a dark place. I can't see where."

Misty relayed the information, and Luke cursed. "Anybody else? Anybody get anything that would help us find her?" Luke glanced around the table.

"I saw the dark place," said Misty, "but I didn't recognize the building."

"A building?" Luke was scrolling through his cell to his police contact at New Orleans PD.

"To me, it seemed like an abandoned school," said Casey, "but I couldn't be sure."

Claire nodded. "Casey is right. The basement of a school where children hang out and do drugs."

"Lukey, what did you feel?" asked Misty.

"Missing persons, please." With his cell to his ear, Luke was on his feet pacing. "I saw smoke and could smell weed. A lot of drugs wherever she is."

"Oh, my," said Gran. "I don't want Rowanne near boys with drugs."

"Believe me, Gran," said Luke. "Neither do I. If she got mixed up with kids like that, Sam will never forgive me, and I will never forgive myself." He straightened against the island once he was connected to missing persons.

Luke explained to Lieutenant White that his niece had run away. "Yes, I can be there in half an hour."

"I'll go with you," said Misty getting up.

"Can I come?" asked Casey. "I want to see inside the police station."

Luke ended the call, waved them to follow, and picked up the truck keys from the table in the hall. "Grab your coats, and let's go. I want the whole New Orleans police force out looking for her ASAP."

New Orleans PD

Lieutenant White greeted Misty, Luke, and Casey with a smile as they entered his office. They had helped him with a couple of cases, and now it was his turn to help them.

"Have a seat, and we'll sort this out." He typed a few keystrokes and began asking the questions to fill out the report. "Let's start with your niece's full name."

"Rowanne Maisy Hyslop."

"Date of birth?"

Luke had to phone his grandmother to get that, and the Lieutenant filled it in. "So… she's sixteen years old, and how would you describe her?"

Luke looked to Misty for the description. "Five feet tall, slim, short red hair."

"Eye color?"

"Dark brown," said Misty. "For such pale skin, her eyes are very dark."

The lieutenant nodded. "And what was she last seen wearing?"

"That's the part we don't know," said Luke. "She left during the night, and we didn't see what she had on."

"But she probably had her jacket on," said Misty, "because it would be cold in the middle of the night. So, I'd guess, black leather jacket, torn jeans, and scuffed army boots."

Luke nodded. "I agree. That sounds about right."

Casey said. "Yesterday she was wearing a black t-shirt with a pentacle on the front. Doesn't mean she's wearing it now."

"But she might have grabbed the same one," said Misty. "Or slept in her clothes for a quick getaway."

When the report was finished, White printed a copy

for Luke to sign.

"Do you know of any abandoned schools around the city?" asked Misty.

"Why do you ask, Madam Le Jeune? Did you have a vision of her whereabouts? asked White.

"Very cloudy, sir. I'm not sure of anything at this point, but I intend to go home and try with a piece of her clothing, that is if she left anything behind. What we did see was possibly an old abandoned school where kids gather in the basement to do drugs."

"We think she headed for the bus terminal and got sidetracked or taken by other kids," said Luke. "I know you'll check, busses, trains, planes, etc."

"That's usually the first thing we do," said the Lieutenant, "along with hospitals, and accident reports."

Luke let out a breath. "My brother is ill and recovering from major surgery. He entrusted me with Rowanne's care until he was up and around. I'm not feeling good about this at all."

"We will use all our resources and do our best to find her," said the Lieutenant. "I have your number."

Luke sat behind the wheel of the Ford SUV in the police station parking lot. "My first inclination is to drive around looking for her, but that may be pointless if she's inside a building. We should go home, and I'll contact the various school boards and get a list of schools that are closed. Then we'll check them one by one."

"You are the sensible one, sweetheart. Let's do that."

"I could walk where she might have walked during the night and see what she passed," said Casey. "Might see something or pick up a vibe."

"Uh-huh," said Luke. "Appreciate anything you could do, Casey. I know you didn't like her much. She's going through a terrible rebellious teen stage right now."

Casey grinned. "I might have been a little like her myself a couple of years ago."

Nine Saint Gillian Street

Luke jogged straight to his room, sat down at his desk, and opened up his laptop. He dove into finding what schools were closed or abandoned in the city, and while he narrowed them down, kept up a running conversation with himself so he wouldn't lose his mind.

"If she walked there, it can't be too far. But what if the boys had a vehicle? Then that wouldn't be true at all. Shit."

Sam's going to kill me.

Maybe Casey will find something.

Angelique and Luke's Gran set up a hoodoo altar in the front parlor and were scribing and burning candles. They took turns chanting spells and petitioning the goddess for the return of a lost loved one.

Lost loved one
Far from home
Now is not the time to roam

Goddess of the sun and moon
Bring Rowanne back home soon
Grant my plea by setting sun
Candles burn
My spell is done
So mote it be.

Casey snapped Hoo's leash onto his collar and struck out on his own to walk the neighborhood. "Let's go find Rowanne, Hoo."

He didn't particularly like her, but she was a defenseless girl out on the streets alone. He remembered what it felt like to be scared of everything and everybody when he ran away from his father in George West, south Texas.

He wouldn't wish that on anyone.

Misty and Claire searched Rowanne's room to see if she had left anything personal behind. All of her clothes were gone from the closet, and the door stood open.

Claire made the bed while they searched and found the girl's athame under her pillow. "Oh, look what I found."

"Fantastic, Mother. We can use that. She probably touched it just last night."

"We'll use the front parlor where Angelique is already set up," said Claire.

By the time they reached the bottom of the stairs, Michele, Diana, and Charlotte had arrived for class and were hanging their coats up.

Diana noticed the candles in the parlor. "Is something happening?"

"Rowanne has run away," said Claire. "We're going to have a circle right now with her athame. It's the only thing she left behind."

"She ran away?" Charlotte sounded stressed. "So soon? She didn't give y'all a chance to get to know her."

"Where's Casey?" asked Diana.

"He took Hoo out to look around the neighborhood for Rowanne."

Diana smiled. "He's a good person."

Misty nodded. "Casey has a pure heart and the best of intentions. He gets that from Blaine, his guardian."

"Come in, girls." Claire motioned them into the front parlor. "We'll do this before we start class."

"This is important," said Charlotte. "We have to find her."

"Her great gran is very upset," whispered Misty. "Let's try extra hard for her."

Michele nodded her dark head. "We will."

Iberville Area. New Orleans

Rowanne woke with a terrible headache and a burning sore spot on the side of her neck. She moaned, and in her foggy reality, thought she was in bed on Saint Gillian Street.

When the stink of her surroundings hit her nostrils and filled her with repulsion, she came fully awake, and the realization of what had happened in the night hit her brain. She let out a scream.

The room was pitch black, but other people were close to her. She could feel them, sense them, but mostly smell them.

Launching to her feet, she tried to run. Something held her back, and she fell to the floor with a thud.

Someone laughed. The voice sounded familiar. Could have been one of the boys from the bus shelter.

The pain in her ankle ripped through her, and warm liquid heat dribbled down onto her bare foot.

Where are my boots?

Rowanne reached down and felt the iron cuff around her ankle. Blood was seeping out from underneath the cuff where she'd ripped the skin. She felt along the chain to see where it went, and it attached to a ring bolted into the floor.

I'm a prisoner.

She sat down, buried her face in her hands, and began to cry. "Let me go. I want to go home."

Someone shone a light in her eyes, and she couldn't see who it was. "You ain't going home, red. We're selling you for big bucks. You the real deal. Know how much we get for genuine virgins?"

"I'm not," Rowanne lied. "I've done it dozens of times."

One of the gangers laughed. "I just bet you have."

I need my wand.

She groped around for her backpack, and it wasn't near her. Not within reach. "I need my backpack," she said.

"You don't need nothing, babyface. Man coming soon to pick your sweet ass up and lay a lot of cash on us. He loves it when we find him somebody fresh as you."

"You guys are going to jail," hollered Rowanne. "You can't take people from the bus shelter."

The kid chuckled. "Oh, no? Tell that to the man. We do it all the time."

Nine Saint Gillian Street

Casey returned home from his walk without finding anything. No trace of Rowanne anywhere he and Hoodoo had walked. Maybe if Hoo had been a bloodhound, they would have discovered which way Rowanne went. He took Hoo's leash off and hung it on the hook in the front closet.

"Anything?" Diana asked. She was sitting in the front parlor with the rest of the women.

Casey shook his head. "What are y'all doing?"

"Using the athame," said Misty. "We each tried but didn't get much from it."

"I'll try," said Casey. "Give me a minute to catch my breath." He hung up his jacket, then sat next to Diana at the round table Misty used for customer readings. He picked up the athame and ran his thumb over the blade. "Can't believe she left this behind. Beautiful handle."

"It is a lovely one," said Claire. "Perhaps it was a

gift."

Casey took a few deep breaths then held the curved knife in his hands. He closed his eyes and tried to picture Rowanne's face. Mostly a grumpy face, but she had smiled once or twice.

After a couple of minutes of clearing his thoughts and sinking into a state of absolute concentration, Casey saw a pair of army boots thrown in the trash. The next thing he saw was even more frightening. In his mind's eye, he saw a slim ankle with an iron cuff and chain attached. He opened his eyes, his breath coming in rapid gasps.

Misty poured him some water. "What, sweetheart? Was it bad?"

"They took her boots off and chained her to a ring in the floor. She's bleeding."

Diana gasped. "Where is she? We have to find her."

Luke came galloping down the staircase with a printed list in his hand. "These are three of the schools now closed. You girls have lived in the city for most of your lives. Do you know of any closed or abandoned schools?"

"I went to Catholic School," said Michele. "I don't know of too many schools, and none that are closed."

"Which ones are on your list?" asked Charlotte. "I know of one a few blocks from where I work that's all boarded up."

"Casey and I will go check that one first. Then we'll do the other three I have on the list from the school board. You ladies stay here in case Rowanne calls for help."

"I should come," said Misty. "Y'all might need me."

Broadmoor

Luke started in Broadmoor district following the little map Charlotte had sketched for him before they left home.

"That's it there, sugar." Misty pointed to an old elementary school with boarded-up windows. The doors were blocked, and not a single soul was in sight.

"This building is sitting right out in the open," said Luke. "People in the neighborhood would see kids or gangers going in and out, and they'd report it in a nanosecond. I'll look in a couple of basement windows, but I don't think this is it."

"I'm not getting any vibes," said Misty. "It feels completely deserted."

Luke circled the building peering in all the windows that weren't completely covered. He got down on his knees at three different spots, and all he saw in the basement were cobwebs. Not a sound was coming from inside. Kids weren't that quiet.

Cross one off the list.

Iberville Area

Rowanne had to pee. She asked one of the boys if she could use the bathroom, and he laughed in her face.

"Ain't no hotel, sister. You can take a piss when the man comes for you and not before."

"But, I have to go now."

"I said *no.*" He backhanded her across the face and hollered at her. "Shut up."

Her face stung where the prick smacked her, and Rowanne sobbed. She'd never been so scared. All she wanted was to go home. She'd even behave perfectly for Uncle Luke if he came to save her. She swore to herself to be a better person... if only she got the chance.

A finger of light poked through one of the boarded-up windows. There was a crack in the plywood, and she could see daylight outside. She had no idea of the time, but her stomach growled like an angry grizzly. She was hungry and remembered a Snickers bar in the bottom of her backpack. If only they'd give it back to her.

Now that there was a glimmer of light and her eyes had become accustomed to the dimness, she could see her surroundings. It had all the ear markings of a school gym, but an old one. One that had survived a war.

A basketball hoop hung crookedly from the end wall. The other walls were tagged with spray-paint graffiti. Blankets and backpacks marked off each kid's territory, and there were a lot of kids there. Twenty or thirty, at least. Most of them about her age but a few older.

This must be where homeless kids hang out.

"If this is a school, there are bathrooms. That kid is full of shit. He just can't be bothered taking me."

Rowanne sat for at least another half hour, then the kid that snatched her from the bus stop walked across the gym with another guy. A tall man in a suit who looked a little older than her daddy.

He smiled down on her. "Aren't you the pretty one?" He pointed at the cuff on her ankle, and the ganger kid undid it and pulled her up onto her feet.

"You're moving on, Red. Enjoy your new life." The ganger kid laughed like crazy, and she wanted to zap him with her wand.

"Can I please bring my backpack and my clothes?"

"Of course, you can, dear." He turned to the kid. "Give me her stuff—all of it."

"Yes, sir." The kid ran somewhere, then came back with her suitcase and her backpack.

"Thank you." The man turned to Rowanne and spoke in a soft voice, "I want you to be comfortable, dear. Why don't you tell me your name?"

"Rowanne."

"That's a lovely name." He flashed her a perfect set of teeth. "Well now, Rowanne, let's get you out of this nasty place, and the first thing we'll do is get you something to eat."

Rowanne nodded. The mention of food should have cheered her a little, but it didn't. She didn't want to go anywhere with this man.

Mid-City District

The next school on Luke's list was in Mid-City. He drove around the block a couple of times before he spotted it.

The schoolyard was large and well-treed, and the school itself sat near the back of the property. What used to be a lawn was now a field of brown weeds. Surrounded by a sturdy wrought iron fence, the gate at the sidewalk was closed and padlocked. He couldn't drive in. He'd have to park and walk.

Luke pulled over to the curb and shut off the truck engine. Misty unbuckled her seat belt and made ready to get out and come with.

"I'd be happier if you stayed here, sweetheart. Who knows what I'll find in there."

"Exactly. That's why I should come and protect you."

"I have a gun."

"I have a wand."

Luke smiled. "All right. Come on. But if I find a way to get inside, I might send you back to the truck to wait for me."

"Deal."

Luke fiddled with the padlock, and his pick set wasn't working. "We'll have to climb over. Why don't you wait in the truck?"

Misty whipped out her wand, focused on the padlock, and mumbled a few words.

Keeper of the gate beware
I need to pass with cause and care
Don't lock me out
Don't lock me in
I have no key
I have no pin
Grant me access
Hear my call
Hasp and lock

You may now fall
So mote it be.

The padlock fell to the ground with the chain on top of it. Misty lifted the latch and opened the gate for Luke.

He rolled his eyes. "Uh-huh."

Luke held Misty's hand as they walked around the outside of the school. No sounds came from inside, and there was no visible entry or exit point. Everything had been carefully locked up and secured.

If kids were running in and out of this building, they were doing it invisibly.

Not this school.

Black Pearl District

The last school on Luke's list was close to the Mississippi. He parked at the curb, and he and Misty walked up to the building. No fence and not yet boarded up. A few broken windows, but it appeared that the city hadn't swooped in to officially close it down. There was nobody around, and they could clearly see through the windows there was no one inside.

"That was the last one, Misty."

"Let's go home. Maybe the Fates will send us something."

Nine Saint Gillian Street

Back home, Luke was disappointed with their findings and depressed. They hadn't come up with a single clue.

His worst fear was that Rowanne was already dead, and no matter how hard they tried to find her, they were already too late.

He tried to banish negative thoughts from his mind, but he'd been a cop or a Texas Ranger for most of his life and knew the stats. As the minutes and hours ticked by, the chances of finding Rowanne became slimmer and slimmer.

"Do you want me to call Leo and tell him we can't make dinner at Casey's?" asked Misty.

"Oh, damn it all, Mist. I forgot all about dinner with Leo. I'll check in with Lieutenant White, then shower and get ready. We have to eat, so we'll meet him. We can take another drive around the city on the way home. Maybe we'll come up with something."

Casey was on kitchen duty, helping Angelique with dinner. "Did you find anything?" he asked.

"No. Checked all the schools on the list and nothing," said Luke. "The Lieutenant didn't call?"

Claire set down her mug. "No. Nothing yet, I'm afraid. The girls are upset. Even though Rowanne treated them badly, they don't want her to be in danger."

"Those three girls are empathetic," said Misty. "They have fine qualities for young women."

Casey nodded his head.

Upstairs, Luke stripped down for his shower, and before going into the ensuite, he called Lieutenant White in missing persons for an update.

"I'm sorry, there's nothing new, Ranger Hyslop."

"Should we be going to the media with her picture?"

"If she doesn't come back by tonight of her own free will, I'm planning on doing a broadcast tomorrow. Perhaps you could make the appeal."

"Of course, call me in the morning when the arrangements have been made."

"I'll be in touch."

Clancy's Restaurant. New Orleans

Leo Pinoit hadn't yet arrived when Luke and Misty were seated at their table at the popular eatery. The hostess left them with menus and removed the reserved sign. A few moments later, a waiter took their drink order: a beer for Luke, and a bottle of Merlot for Misty. Still no Leo.

They studied the menu for twenty minutes, and Luke was in the process of pouring Misty a second glass of wine when he said, "Should we call Leo? He's very late, and I want to order. I'm about to starve."

"I'll call," said Misty. She scrolled to Leo's contact information and waited for Leo to answer.

Craig Gibson, Leo's assistant, answered in a panic. He was screaming and crying at the same time. "You must come and help me, Madam. Leo has been murdered in his bed. Please, please, come immediately."

"We're coming," said Misty. She emptied her wine glass and stood. "Leo is dead. Craig needs us."

"What?" Misty caught him off guard when he was in deep thought about Rowanne.

"Craig is overwrought. We have to go."

Luke groaned, his empty stomach not at all pleased with the change of plans. He tossed the money for their drinks on the table, and they left in a hurry.

Misty punched Leo's address into the GPS, and Luke got them going.

"What did Craig tell you on the phone?" asked Luke.

"Just what I told you. Leo is dead in his bed."

"Do you think Marvin Downes took a second shot at him?"

Misty shrugged. "Maybe I'll know more when I'm at the scene."

Marigny District

First Response had already arrived when they pulled up to the curb down the road. An ambulance, two squad cars, and a fire truck took up most of the block. Luke had to park Misty's Expedition close to the corner. He took her hand, and they hurried along the sidewalk.

A uniformed officer stood on the front step of Leo's fashionable townhouse guarding the door and protecting the crime scene.

Luke held up his creds, and the uniform looked twice. "Why would a Texas Ranger be here?"

"I'm a friend of Leo's and spoke to him a few days ago about another attempt on his life. I'm here to help the officer in charge if needed."

He gave Misty the once over. "And who might you

be little lady? You a Texas Ranger too?"

"Mystere LeJeune," said Misty.

The uniformed officer's eyes widened, and he stepped back to let her pass. "Welcome, Madam. You are as beautiful as your reputation says you are."

Misty smiled at him. "Thank you for that. Very kind."

Once they stepped into the foyer, a bleary-eyed Craig came running towards them with arms outstretched. "I'm going to die," he howled. "I'm going to succumb this very night."

Misty hugged him. "How about we step into the kitchen, and you can collect your thoughts while Luke sees what he can find out?"

"Yes, shall we? I could use a moment."

Misty followed Craig into the kitchen, and Luke sought out the victim and the forensic team. He wanted to see the body and the crime scene. You could learn a lot from the scene if you knew what you were looking for.

Upstairs in the master suite, the Medical Examiner was hovering over Leo's body, taking his temperature to determine the time of death.

"How long?" asked Luke.

"Who are you, sir?" asked the ME's assistant.

Again, Luke held up his creds. "I was supposed to have dinner with Leo tonight. My date and I were waiting for him at Clancy's when Craig gave us the news."

"No discernible cause of death at this point, sir. We'll have to wait for the autopsy, I'm afraid."

Luke nodded. Leo looked peaceful enough in death.

"Check for poison. It wouldn't be the first time Leo was poisoned since the new year."

Nine Saint Gillian Street

Misty nuked up leftovers for her and Luke, and they settled at the dining room table. "What did the crime scene tell you?"

Luke ate for a few minutes before he was ready to take a break and speak between bites. "Nothing. We'll have to wait for the forensic team to give us a place to start."

"Can you start if they don't ask you to help with the investigation?"

"Formally, no, but we can poke around on our own."

Misty smiled. "We can."

Luke frowned. "I'm sorry, Mist, but you understand that my priority is finding Rowanne, right?"

"Of course, sugar," Misty said, reaching for her napkin. "Your niece is priority one."

CHAPTER FOUR

Saturday, February 4th.

<u>The Hilton Hotel</u>

"This is your room, Rowanne. You'll be sharing with Bridgette, Mia, and Evey. Make room in the closet, girls, for Rowanne's things. She's your new roommate."

"Hi," said one of the girls. She sat on the bed with a lot of pillows propped up behind her, painting her nails.

The man left the room and closed the door behind him.

Rowanne picked up her backpack and took it over to the table by the window. The girls looked like they were having a slumber party, not victims of abduction. "What are y'all doing? Don't you want to get away from that man?"

"Can't get away," the one painting her nails said.

"Why not?"

"You'll find out."

"My uncle will find me. I won't be here long enough to find out anything."

The girls laughed at her.

"I'm Mia," said the thin one with the dark hair. "That's Bridgette doing her nails, and Evey is sleeping."

Rowanne tried the door, and it opened. Peeking out, she thought that maybe this would be easier than she anticipated. "I don't see anybody in the hall. I'm outta here."

"Not a good idea," said Mia, shaking her head. "They watch us all the time. I wouldn't try it."

"What'll they do to me?" asked Rowanne. "Kill me?"

"Trust us," Bridgette said, frowning. "There are many things worse than death."

"Like what?"

Bridgette screwed the lid back onto her nail polish and shrugged. "Stuff you wish you never knew about."

Rowanne dug her extra wand out of her backpack and showed the girls. "Let them try to hurt me. I'm a witch. I have powers."

Mia giggled. "Good one. Why don't you transport us to a nice beach in Florida?"

"I can't transport people—at least not yet—but I know someone who can."

"Uh-huh." Bridgette pointed at a stack of books on the nightstand. "You'll have lots of time to live in a fantasy world while you're here."

"I'm not reading a fucking book. I'm getting out of here."

Rowanne walked over to the house phone and picked it up. "Does this work?"

"Disconnected."

"Who is the guy who brought me here?"

"His name is Malcolm."

"Malcolm, what? Does he have a last name?"

Mia shrugged. "Don't know. We only go by first names."

"Why do y'all take orders from him? You can't just stay in this room and never leave. What's going on?"

"You'll find out soon enough."

"I'm not waiting around long enough to find out."

Rowanne shrugged into her backpack, picked up her suitcase, and went out the door. She didn't know where the elevator was, so ran to her right. She found three doors at the end of the corridor. She was at them when someone grabbed her from behind and picked her up.

"No, you don't, little Red. We have plans for you."

"Let me go," Rowanne hollered, and the kid who had hold of her clamped his hand over her mouth.

He carried her like a sack of potatoes and shoved her back into the room with the other girls. "Don't do that again, or you'll be one sorry little girl."

Rowanne reached into her pocket and curled her fingers around her wand.

Fever comes when witches call
Burn his ass
And scald his balls

She repeated it twice more and focused on his ass as he headed for the door.

"Ow." The guy hollered. He jumped up and down a couple of times, then ran into the bathroom, and they could hear the water running.

"What's wrong with him?" asked Bridgette.

"I fried his balls," said Rowanne.

Mia giggled. "That's funny."

"You really *are* a witch?" asked Evey, the one who'd been sleeping.

"Yep. Real live hereditary witch."

Nine Saint Gillian Street

Luke tossed and turned most of the night, and when he woke, Misty was gone. He sat on the side of the bed with his head in his hands wondering what kind of new hell the day would unleash.

He'd talked to Sam on the phone the night before, and his bullheaded brother was insisting on driving down from Baton Rouge and doing the appeal himself this morning.

Guilt over losing Rowanne was eating Luke alive.

He pulled on a pair of jeans and headed downstairs. Casey caught up with him on the back porch and lit up a smoke.

"What time is Rowanne's father arriving?"

"Soon, I think," said Luke. "I have to shower and get ready to take him to the TV station."

Casey nodded and didn't say anything, but Luke

could tell the kid was deep in thought. Casey was sharp for seventeen, and he was working diligently to gain control of his powers.

"Did you have any thoughts or dreams of where they had taken her?" asked Luke

Casey shrugged. "I keep seeing water. It's like she can see the Gulf from where she is."

Luke listened for a clue. Anything. He needed something.

"If she sees water, she's not in a dark school anymore," said Casey. "They moved her, but I don't know where or why."

"There is so much water throughout the city," said Luke, "but I thank you for trying, Casey. You've been great."

"No problem." Casey put out his smoke. "We should eat breakfast soon if you have to go downtown."

"I don't know if I can choke anything down, but I should try. It could be another long nightmarish day."

Breakfast was almost over when the doorbell rang, and Hoodoo barked and ran into the foyer. Luke hopped up from the dining room table to let his brother in. He opened the heavy carved door and stepped back, shocked by Sam's thin, sallow face.

How much weight has he lost?

Luke hugged him and tried not to let his worry show. "Come, join us for breakfast before we go. We have an hour."

Sam nodded. "Coffee only, thanks. I ate before I left."

Luke sized up his brother and figured Sam should be eating a lot more. He was down at least thirty pounds since the last time he'd seen him. They shared the same build, five ten and a solid hundred and ninety-five pounds. Sam had to be less than one-sixty.

"Is there any news?" asked Sam. "I know you'd have called if there was, but I have to ask. I'm losing my mind thinking about my little girl lost in the city somewhere."

"Nothing new."

If the people holding her captive moved her like Casey thought, several things could be happening—and none of them were good. *I don't want Sam to know about any of them.*

Luke introduced Sam to Misty, her mother, Angelique, and Casey. Sam held his grandmother in a long hug before he sat down at the table.

"Would you like a piece of cornbread with your coffee?" asked Misty. "Angelique just took it out of the pan."

"No thanks. Coffee is fine."

Luke's cell rang, and he stepped into the kitchen to answer. "Lieutenant White, do you have something?"

"No, I'm afraid not. I wanted to be sure you were bringing pictures we could use."

"My brother was supposed to bring them. I'll make sure he has them. We're leaving shortly, and we'll meet you at the TV station."

Luke returned to the dining room and asked, "Did you

bring the pictures, Sam? The Lieutenant was double-checking before we left for the studio."

Sam nodded. "I have several recent ones in the car."

WWX TV station. Downtown New Orleans

Luke kept a sharp eye on his brother as Sam checked his notes. A woman fussed with his dark, curly hair, and he waved her away. His hair was the last thing Sam was concerned with.

There wasn't a hint of color in Sam's face. He had the pasty countenance of someone who rose from his hospital bed way too soon.

Misty squeezed Luke's hand. "No. He doesn't look strong enough to do this."

He still wasn't used to Misty being able to read his mind.

The bright lights came on, and the woman in charge gave the signal. She introduced the problem, and then the camera panned over to Sam. As she asked him the first question, all of Sam's strength seemed to seep out of him. Even sitting in the club chair provided, he looked like he still might hit the floor.

The moderator seemed to realize the same thing and kept things going. "I understand you've been ill and not long out of the hospital, Mr. Hyslop. Thank you for coming to talk to us about your daughter, Rowanne."

Luke's chest was tight as he and Misty stood at the side of the stage watching. His brother got back into the conversation for a bit. He managed to say a few words about Rowanne and how much she meant to him before his eyes rolled back and he slumped sideways.

"Call an ambulance," hollered Luke, as he ran towards his brother. "He's not strong enough to do this." He turned towards the camera, not knowing if they were still filming or not. "If you see the girl in the picture on your screen, please, please call the hotline number. Her absence is literally killing my brother."

When the light on the camera went out, the woman swallowed, looking shaken. "That should get the calls started."

Five minutes later, the paramedics arrived and whisked an unconscious Sam off to University Hospital.

Nine Saint Gillian Street

Casey was in the kitchen with Angelique packing salves and healing lotions for shipping when his cell rang. "Diana? Hi."

"Hey, Casey. The girls and I were wondering if y'all needed help looking for Rowanne today? We're not working until tonight on the late shift, and we could come by."

"Thanks," said Casey. "Luke and Misty are at the TV station, making the public appeal. If you're up for it, I'd like to get out of the house and take another shot at tracking her. I've been getting a lot of water images. Maybe we could look along the river and maybe try scrying for her?"

"Of course, we'll pick you up in fifteen minutes."

"Perfect. I'll grab what we need and wait out front."

Casey slid into the backseat with Diana, and Charlotte drove them slowly along Tchoupitoulas Street as it wound along the edge of the Mississippi River. The four of them scanned every building they passed and saw nothing out of the ordinary.

Casey was careful to scrutinize every crowd of tourists on the street looking for any glimpse of the flaming red hair.

"See if there's somewhere to pull over into a parking lot or empty spot, Char. There are miles of riverfront to cover, and I'm hoping we can narrow the area a little using magick."

"Don't forget the other side of the river," said Michele. She rode shotgun and twisted back to talk to them.

"We can double back and cross over on the I-90 bridge," said Charlotte, "when we finish looking on this side."

"There's a spot up further where I know I can pull to the side," Charlotte said. "What are we doing?"

Casey held up the pendulum, the map of the waterfront he printed off, his bag of crystals, and the three strands of red hair he'd found on Rowanne's pillow. "We're scrying."

Hilton Hotel

Rowanne took her turn in the shower, washed her hair,

and changed into clean clothes. Her tops were a little rumpled from bouncing around in her suitcase, but at this point, she didn't care what her clothes looked like. The only thing she wanted was to get away from these people and go home.

Food had been sent up to their room. Despite not liking breakfast, she'd cleaned up every scrap of the ham and eggs on her plate.

Mia, Bridgette, and Evey occupied their time with nail polish and curling irons, but Rowanne was focused on getting free and running to the nearest police station.

"I don't understand why y'all don't want to get out of here and like... call the cops."

Mia shrugged. "Alive here is better than dead in an alley. Bridgette tried to run away three times, and they punished her."

"How?" asked Rowanne. "What did they do to you?"

"You don't want to know," Bridgette said.

Rowanne sighed. "I *do* want to know. I want to know what the risks are before I try again."

Bridgette stood up, turned her back to Rowanne, and pulled up her top.

Rowanne sucked in a breath when she saw how red and sore the welts looked on Bridgette's back. "What if I could get us all out of here? Would y'all go with me?"

Evey shook her head. "It's not possible. We're trapped, and it's for life, and there's no way out."

"My uncle Luke is a Texas Ranger, and he's smart. His girlfriend is the most powerful witch in New Orleans.

They won't stop looking for me. When they come, I need you girls to be ready to escape."

Evey gave Rowanne an unconvincing smile. "If your people come to save us, we'll be ready to escape. It's just… they won't come."

Rowanne didn't believe that. Sure, she'd been a giant pain in the ass, but they would search for her. Uncle Luke would never give up. "We need a phone, a computer, some way to get a message out."

Mia giggled. "You go, girl."

University Hospital

Luke and Misty waited while Sam was examined by the doctor on call in the cardiology unit. They'd been stuck in the waiting room drinking lousy coffee for almost two hours when a nurse came to tell them that Sam had been admitted. The heart doctor had sedated him, forcing him to rest, and they wouldn't be able to see him until the following day."

"Thank you," said Luke. He handed the nurse his card. "Please call if there's any change, or if Sam wants me."

The nurse glanced at the card in her hand. "Of course, Ranger Hyslop. I'll call you."

He turned to leave and then thought of something else. "Oh, and nurse? His daughter, Rowanne, is currently missing. If he asks about her or wants an update on her case, please let him know I'm working with the police, and I'll keep him posted."

The nurse nodded a second time. "Don't worry. I'll tell him."

On the way home, Misty said, "I've been getting strong vibes from Leo. He's trying to tell me something."

"You don't usually communicate with the spirit world, do you, sweetheart?"

"Not as a rule, except for Daddy, of course, but if Leo is reaching out for any reason, I want to help him."

"Perhaps your father can help you with that," said Luke. "Him being on the same ghostly plane and all."

Misty smiled. "You are so smart, Lukey. One of the things I love about you."

"Are there any others?" Luke reached across the console for her hand.

"Many others. Too numerous to mention."

Luke chuckled. "You cheer me, sweetheart, even in my darkest hour, and this seems like one of the darkest since..." Luke took a couple of deep breaths and tried his best to smile. "I love you, Misty, so very much."

"Ditto."

Marigny District

Misty called Craig before leaving Saint Gillian Street to ask permission to come over with her mother. He readily agreed. Craig knew what a big believer Leo had been in Misty's powers and supported any idea that might help him find peace. What Misty didn't mention, was that she'd be bringing her father, Josiah LeJeune, along to talk to Leo's spirit if Leo hadn't moved on yet.

Chances were good that Leo was still around if something blocked his path into the beyond. Being murdered could do that to a person. They'd delay leaving this world as long as possible, hoping for revenge or retribution.

Misty parked the Ford truck in the driveway of the townhouse and turned off the engine. She turned to speak to the back seat. "Are you ready, Daddy?"

"I'm ready, child. If your friend hasn't made a quick exit into the spirit world and can give us a clue as to who killed him, I shall find out."

Misty smiled. "Thank you, Daddy. If he was poisoned, like Luke and I think he was, he may have died in minutes."

"Even so, darling child, I would have tried to leave a clue."

"Baloney, Daddy. You never left us a clue. We didn't know who killed you until you got around to telling me later that it was that horrid Matthias Rush."

"I thought it was obvious," her father said. "The desire to possess the LeJeune Book of Shadows has been responsible for many deaths over the years. The fact that y'all didn't put that together was astonishing to me."

Misty rolled her eyes. "Oh, Daddy."

Claire ended the conversation with a wave of her hand. "Enough, you two. Let's go inside. As soon as Craig gives us a place to set up, I'll summon Leo."

Craig answered the door on the first ring of the bell and greeted them somberly, almost with reverence. He held a wad of tissue in his hand and dabbed at his red eyes. "Please come in. I'm honored you'd do this for Leo to try to find his killer. How can I help?"

"We need a table, and that's about all." Misty's mother patted the side of her floral tote. "I brought my own candle and everything else I might need."

"Will the dining room suit you, ladies?" asked Craig.

He led the way into the lavishly appointed room hung with tapestries and expensive artwork and flicked the wall switch. The oversized chandelier burst to life and almost blinded them with its crystal brilliance.

"This is fine," said Misty, blinking a couple of times. "Will you join us, Craig? Leo might feel more comfortable if you were here at the table."

"I'd love to be part of your little… gathering. If you don't think I'll intrude or block signals from beyond or anything."

Misty wondered how old Craig was. Tall and slim with a handsome face and perfectly cut and styled silver hair, it was hard to be certain. In his right ear, he wore a diamond stud.

Had Craig been more to Leo than his faithful personal assistant? They might never know.

Misty breathed deeply, in and out, centering her energy as her mother set up.

Claire unpacked her pretty, floral bag and began by smoothing out the black satin altar cloth. She placed the cloth across the center of the table, then placed the scribed candle on top. Once she had the candle burning, she asked

Craig to dim the chandelier and close the drapes.

A soft golden glow filled the room with warmth and a welcoming ambiance. Craig sat silently at the end of the table, mesmerized, while Claire called to Leo.

> *Robbed of life*
> *And mystic planes traveling*
> *Return to us*
> *To aid in unraveling*
> *The violence against you*
> *For we can't defend*
> *Without a clue*
> *Name enemy, dear friend.*
> *Spirit speak*
> *So we may hear*
> *Who took the life*
> *Of one we hold dear*

Claire sat silently with her eyes closed.

The candle flickered for a few moments, then a bitterly cold wind whipped through the room, blowing the drapes wildly about and rattling the fine china in the sideboard.

The bulbs in the chandelier burst in unison, popping like cherry bombs on the Fourth of July. Tiny shards of glass rained down on the table like icy confetti. The room grew quiet as an eerie glow appeared in the upper corner of the room.

A tiny mewling noise came from Craig as he focused on the apparition.

"Leo, is that you?" asked Misty. "Talk to him,

Daddy."

"Who killed you, Leo?" her father asked. "Do you know?"

Only Misty and Claire could hear Josiah speaking to Leo. The ectoplasm high in the corner swirled as the rhyme floated on the air.

My spirit rages
Through the ages
Love is false
In early stages
The truth appears
In the pages

Claire held onto the fluttering pages of her notebook as the wind whistled through the room.

Leo was gone.

"That was frightening," said Craig. Visibly shaken, he rose to his feet and stared at all the broken glass strewn on the table. "I'll clean that up. Would you ladies like tea?"

Misty's mother nodded and sank deeper into her chair. "Please, yes. That was quite draining."

"It certainly was, and disappointing too. Leo didn't even say anything."

Misty shifted the candle to the table and started folding up her mother's altar. "Oh, he did. You just didn't hear him."

"He spoke?" Craig looked unconvinced. "May I know what he said? Did he ask about me? Is he missing me?"

Misty smiled up at Craig. "I'm sure he is, but he didn't say. He spoke a rhyme. Mother wrote it down."

Claire read from her notes, and Craig shrugged. "That doesn't sound like Leo. He was never a fan of poetry. Are you sure it was him?"

"I'm sure," said Josiah. "It was Leo."

"It was Leo," said Claire.

Craig shrugged. "One moment, I'll get the tea."

Hilton Hotel

The door of their hotel room opened, and the man who'd bought Rowanne from the abandoned school street kids, Malcolm, came in with a big smile on his face. "Time to go girls." He checked each one of them to make sure they were dressed. He'd provided each of them with a designer outfit he wanted them to wear. "Wonderful. You all look wonderful."

Rowanne never wore lipstick and felt ridiculous. Mia said she had to wear it, or she'd be in big trouble.

There was no trouble bigger than this.

Malcolm winked at her, and Rowanne's skin crawled. "Now, for the sake of your newest roommate, Rowanne, let's have a reminder of our rules when out in public. No making a scene. No speaking to anyone. No furtive glances or doing anything that draws attention to you. All of my men are armed, and none of them will allow you to cause any trouble. If any of you tries, the others will suffer the consequences."

Rowanne said nothing.

Despite his threats, she'd wait for her opening and run like the wind as soon as she had the opportunity. Nobody was going to keep her under their thumb or whip her like they'd whipped the other girls.

She was a witch, stronger, and smarter than the average girl.

One of Malcolm's men opened the door, and they were escorted downstairs, through the lobby and into a waiting limo. Strange. No one seemed to notice four teenaged girls dressed up to walk the red carpet.

We have to get away from these people.

CHAPTER FIVE

Sunday, February 5th.

<u>Nine Saint Gillian Street</u>

Luke paced in the backyard while he smoked. A cold snap had hit Louisiana, and a sprinkling of snow had fallen overnight. It melted right away, but waking up and seeing a thin sheet of white over everything was startling.

He hadn't had an update from Lieutenant White, and that probably meant he had nothing to tell him. Had there been any calls to the hotline? Had anybody seen Rowanne? Were the police chasing down leads? How would he find out?

Luke called the station and spoke to the detective on duty. A Miss Tracey Ulrich.

"This is Texas Ranger, Luke Hyslop. I'm calling to check the status of my niece, Rowanne's case."

"Several phone calls came in after the media appeal, sir, but none of them panned out, I'm sorry to say."

He figured as much. "Could you tell me if the calls were from all over the city or perhaps more heavily concentrated in one general area?"

"Just glancing at the locations, Ranger Hyslop, I'd

have to say most came from the hotel strip in the Quarter."

"Thank you," said Luke. "With nothing else to go on, I'll start there. It could either be a clue or the fact that a busy tourist area has more people to get involved. Either way, it gives me somewhere to focus."

"Good luck, sir. Lieutenant White left your contact info with me. I'll call if there's anything concrete."

"Thank you."

Hoodoo launched off the back porch as Casey joined him outside in their designated smoker's area. "Anything new with Rowanne?" Casey asked.

Luke exhaled heavily. "A few calls came into the hotline from the vicinity of the big hotels. I might take a drive and see if I can find anything."

"We cruised both sides of the river yesterday," said Casey. "We tried scrying for her, but maybe we weren't doing it right because we got nothing."

"I appreciate y'all trying. It's killing me not to know what to do next. This isn't my jurisdiction. I can't insert myself and take over the investigation."

Casey shrugged. "If someone is holding Rowanne against her will, she'll be trying her damndest to get away. It's her nature, and she has a strong will. We should expect a message of some sort. That's what I'm thinking."

Luke nodded. "Who do you see her reaching out to?"

"If I were predicting, I'd say you or your Gran. She's close to your Gran, and your grandmother is a practitioner. She's highly attuned to the vibes."

"You're a clever guy, Casey." Luke gave him a fist

bump. "I'll ask Gran to open herself up for a message from Row. She's depressed about Rowanne running away, and now about Sam's relapse. Focusing on something will give Gran hope."

Country Estate... Location Unknown

Rowanne had no idea where she was or whose house she was in. From the bedroom window, all she could see was a lot of grass, a huge swimming pool with a cover over it and trees. All around the property on every side, trees grew close together like a forest.

If she could see a forest, she had to be out of the city. But where? How would anyone find her if she did run away? She used the bathroom, then checked the other girls, and they were still sleeping. They'd been up all night at the party. The creepiest party she'd ever been to.

The guests were all men, and they stared at her like she was from Mars. Mia, Evey, and Bridgette knew a lot of the other girls and spent time laughing and drinking with their friends. A lot of drugs were available for the girls and all the guests, but she wasn't going to do drugs no matter what these people did to her.

She was a witch and lived in harmony with nature, the universe, and the elements. The goddess would send her a way. All she had to do was wait.

In the meantime, she'd meditate and cleanse her mind. Rid her thoughts of the man who ripped her clothes off as she fought against him, and when he tired of using her, pressed money into her hand and left her crying.

Rowanne picked a spot on the carpet where she could see the sun and sat down cross-legged. She closed her eyes and cleared all negative thoughts from her head the way her great gran had taught her.

Nine Saint Gillian Street

Misty drank tea at the kitchen table with her mother as they tried to decipher Leo's poetic message from the night before.

"What do you think he was telling us, Daddy?"

"He said *pages*," said Josiah, "so that means a letter, a book, something along those lines."

Her mother frowned. "It's too bad he couldn't be more specific. Spirits aren't as focused or forthright in death as they were in life."

"Are you saying I'm more deceptive, my darling?"

"Definitely, you are. You used to be a pussycat, and I could read your every thought."

Josiah's eerie laughter filled the kitchen and gave Misty the shivers.

Misty was getting used to her parents, interacting again. Half the time, she couldn't decide if they were fighting or flirting. Still, she was so thankful to have her mother home and her family back together—even if her father was a ghost.

"What Leo told us does neither us nor the police any good. We have to figure out what it means."

Her mother agreed. "But we have a better chance of finding out the meaning than they do."

"Do you feel like having Italian for lunch, Mother?"

Claire smiled. "I'm craving crab carbonara."

After breakfast, Luke sat in the front parlor with his gran and explained to her what Casey thought might happen. "Casey thinks Rowanne will send a message, and he thought you would be her most likely choice. I want you to be aware of any images or thoughts coming into your mind, Gran. It may be Rowanne calling for help."

Gran nodded her head. "I will focus and be waiting for her message."

Luke squeezed her hand and marveled, as always, at the strength of his grandmother. "In an hour, I'll call the hospital and see if we're allowed to visit Sam."

She sighed, a deep frown marring her beautiful face. "We must get Rowanne home. Sam shouldn't be under this kind of stress in his condition."

"Agreed. The sooner we find Rowanne, the sooner we'll get rid of his stress."

Unable to content himself waiting around for word on his niece, Luke needed to do something positive. He found Casey in the kitchen. "Want to go for a drive?"

"Sure. Do we have a sighting?"

"No. Nothing solid. Since a few of the calls came from the hotel district near the river, I thought we'd take the pictures of Rowanne with us and ask some of the bellmen and registration employees. I'm not good at waiting."

"Yep, I'm up for that. Let me get my jacket."

Riverfront

Luke parked in one of the ramps convenient to several of the large hotels. He and Casey walked from there. They hit the lobbies of all the major hotels on both sides of the street and showed Rowanne's picture to all the registration clerks on duty.

At each location, they left behind one of Luke's cards and a printed picture to show those employees not on shift at the time. They might be wasting their time and energy on old fashioned leg-work, but Luke would slog every street in N'Oleans if it meant getting Rowanne back.

Downe's Italian Eatery

Unable to figure out Leo's cryptic clue without more information, Misty and Claire took a cab to Marvin Downe's restaurant. The hostess seated them and told them about the lunch special. Sadly, not crab carbonara, but Claire toughed it out and ordered the cannelloni.

Misty ordered a bottle of wine and inquired pleasantly as to the proprietor's whereabouts.

"Oh, Mr. Downe is in Italy selecting wine for the restaurant for the coming season. He's been gone for two weeks but expected back soon."

"Thank you." When the server left the table, Misty leaned close to her mother. "If that's true, Marvin Downes didn't kill Leo. We can eliminate him. We need a new suspect."

"But Leo was positive Marvin Downes poisoned him the first time," said Claire. "Could he have been mistaken?"

"Maybe. It could have seemed that way because they ate in his restaurant, but it could have been accidental, or maybe someone else entirely."

"Who else would want him out of the way?"

Misty shrugged. "We should talk to the people he worked with at the magazine."

"Maybe someone else was angry after receiving a dreadful review. We should talk to his editor."

"Tomorrow is Monday. We'll make an appointment."

"You'll have to do it, darling. I have classes."

Misty smiled at her mother. "I keep forgetting you're a dedicated educator now."

"I'm not that dedicated. I'm only having a bit of fun."

University Hospital

After several hours of tramping through hotel lobbies, and making little progress finding Rowanne, Luke dropped into the hospital to see his brother before going home.

"I won't stay long," he told Casey as they rode up to Sam's room in the elevator.

"I'm fine. I'll grab a coffee and rest my legs. I thought at least one person would have seen her. Are they all brain dead?"

"Seems like it. People are so apathetic."

Luke left Casey in the waiting area and entered the cardiac unit to see his brother. Sam was awake and seemed more alert, but that was only Luke's impression.

He wasn't a doctor.

Sam's voice was weak. He wasn't projecting much sound, and Luke had to lean close to hear. "Anything, Luke? Has anyone seen her?"

"Everyone's out looking for her, Sam. I'm hoping she'll send a message to Gran or to me."

"How? If someone kidnapped her, the first thing they'd do is take her cell phone away."

"Not that kind of a message," he said, checking that their conversation wouldn't be overheard. "A psychic message."

Sam shook his head. "You don't honestly believe people can do that, do you? Rowanne thinks she has powers because Gran put that in her head, but come on. She's an ordinary, angry teenager who says she has magick so she can feel special."

I don't agree.

Sam pushed the blanket back and glared at the IV stuck in the back of his hand. "I need to get out of here and look for my daughter. I'll go nuts cooped up here, not being able to do anything. Talk to the doctor, Lukey. Make him let me go."

"I'll talk to him, Sam, but I'm sure he'll want you to give it a couple more days. You're not strong enough yet. When I find Rowanne, she's going to need you alive, not lying in a coffin in some funeral home."

Sam smirked. "You're being dramatic, aren't you, Luke?"

"I don't think so. You almost died, Sam. Twice. You

have to give yourself a chance to recover."

"Someone could be hurting her, and I'm lying here doing nothing. She's all I've got."

"I understand. Tomorrow morning, I have an appointment with Lieutenant White. I have a few ideas that I want to run by him. I want the police force exploring every possibility."

"Let me be part of this. I don't want to lie here, worrying."

Luke hated to see Sam so distraught but knew that hospital bed was the only place his brother was well enough to be. "Here's the deal. You lay here for another day and recover, and I'll stop in tomorrow after I've been to headquarters and give you a full report. We can talk to the doctor about your progress and see where we are then, how's that?"

Sam tipped his head back and glared at the ceiling tiles of his room. "Okay. Don't forget."

Country Estate… Location Unknown

Rowanne woke early, showered and dressed, and had gathered the belongings she'd been allowed to keep. The house was quiet, and several times, she'd walked the upstairs hallway listening for male voices on the lower level. There had been some earlier, but they were gone. Her heart thundered as she anticipated her escape attempt. She had to consider everything to ensure her plan worked.

The girls woke one by one, and the first thing they wanted was food. Rowanne followed Evey and Mia downstairs to the kitchen, and she was right, there was no one around.

Where did they all go?

"We should leave now. Nobody is watching us."

"That's because there's nowhere to go. This house is far from everything."

"How far?"

Evey rolled her eyes. "Like… miles and miles. Didn't you pay attention on the drive out here? They're not watching us because they know there's nowhere we can go."

"Well, we can't just stay here. We have to try to get help."

Mia shrugged. "You're assuming we all want help. What if it's better than what's waiting for us back home. What if we're used to this life."

Rowanne hadn't considered that—couldn't grasp that what happened last night was favorable over anything else. How could it be?

"Well, I'm not used to this life, and I never will be. I'll take my chances in the miles and miles of nothing."

Evey shook her head. "Don't. Don't run away. When they catch you, you'll be sorry. Disobeying orders gets you nowhere you want to be. It's better to stay here and stay safe."

Rowanne shook her head. "Do you hear how stupid that sounds. Do you understand that all y'all are brainwashed? Don't give in to them and accept this. Malcolm and his men are selling you for money. That's sex trafficking, and it's a crime. I'm not staying here. I don't take orders from anybody."

With her backpack on her shoulders, Rowanne opened the garden doors at the back of the house and took off running. She couldn't get away from there fast enough. Frigid air filled her lungs and made it hard to breathe as she ran in a straight line right into the trees at the back of the property.

What was on the other side of the forest? It didn't matter. Anything would be better than being held prisoner by the creepy men in suits who controlled the other girls.

Once she reached the trees, Rowanne slowed down to catch her breath and continued walking at a quick pace. The trees were tall and straight and grew close together. There were no paths and nothing telling her which way to go to the closest road.

Leaves and needles crunched under her boots as she trod along, happy to be free, but determined to make it last. The woodsy smell of the forest filled her with calmness, and for the first time in days, she had hope.

She walked for hours, got as far as she could, and then sat down on a fallen tree to rest. With her eyes open, Rowanne turned her head in a one-eighty and took a mental picture of where she was. Then she closed her eyes, concentrated hard, and sent the picture of the woods to her great-grandmother.

In the past two days, she hadn't been able to center herself enough to access her powers right. But here, surrounded by the security of nature, and her freedom reclaimed, she lowered her guard and focused.

"Help me, Gran. I'm in the woods, and I'm lost."

Nine Saint Gillian Street

Iris Hyslop was in her room lying on her bed. With her eyes closed and her spirit open, she was ready when the picture of the dense woods flashed through her mind. She waited, hoping for more, listening for Rowanne's voice. She heard her great-granddaughter calling for help.

Gran rose, reached for her sweater, and went downstairs to find Luke.

Angelique was busy in the kitchen, boiling crawdads for dinner.

"Has Luke come back yet?" she asked.

"Not yet. Do you need him?"

Iris nodded. "Rowanne contacted me with an impression of her surroundings. I want to tell Luke."

Angelique smiled. "I don't know about Luke, but Madam is parking de truck at de back, right now. She be able to help you, I'm sure."

Minutes later, Misty and Claire came through the back door and met Gran waiting for them.

"Rowanne reached out to me," Gran said. "There were a lot of trees, like in a forest, and she needs help."

"A forest?" Misty pulled her cell phone out of her pocket and called Luke. "Are you home soon?"

"Five minutes away. Why?"

"Your Gran had a vision."

"Coming right now," said Luke.

Louisiana Forest

As the sun went down, Rowanne wondered whether she should keep walking or find a place to spend the night. She'd heard of people lost in the woods, wandering in circles for hours and days. Without the sun to guide her, she had no sense of direction. She decided on finding a hiding spot where she might have a measure of safety from the elements as well as any of Malcolm's men who might pursue her.

The hollow in the trunk of a huge tree was the best spot she could find on short notice. She had to hurry and pick something as the forest was becoming darker and colder by the moment.

Pushing her backpack ahead of her, she crawled over the maze of tangled roots into her hiding place. There was just enough room for her to turn around and sit up. Her hair brushed the top of the opening, and she could barely move her arms without hitting the inside of the tree.

A feeling of dampness seeped under her shirt. She wished she had a jacket. Rowanne's teeth chattered— from the drop in temperature, fear, or possibly from both. As she shivered, she wrapped her arms around herself and tried to conserve her body heat. Ignoring the growling of her stomach, she stayed curled in a ball and closed her eyes.

Each strange sound in the trees surrounding her had her wide-eyed and picturing a black bear or a bobcat coming to tear her to bits. The sounds of night creatures hunting for food was terrifying.

Fallen leaves made a rustling sound as small animals

or rodents scurried past. Owls high above her head flapped their wings with a whirring sound and scared the crap out of her every time they let out a hoot.

"Stop hooting. Y'all are scaring me."

They didn't listen.

Rowanne didn't remember falling asleep but woke startled by a sound close by. She froze, her ears ringing to hear every noise. It wasn't an animal sound—she was pretty sure about that. She retained a mental list of each scrape and rustle and grunt she'd heard earlier, and what she imagined made the sound. Whatever woke her, didn't belong on the list. This was a human sound.

She waited, silent and frozen in the darkness.

Men were talking, and they weren't far away.

They came closer—too close—and she listened. She heard at least three or four different voices as they stomped through the woods with bright flashlight beams arcing ahead of them. Shining the light back and forth, the men searched every inch of the woods. They were looking for her.

They were close, almost on top of her tree hideout when a spider crawled down her arm. Her first reaction was to scream at the top of her lungs.

Don't do it.

She chomped down on her tongue, held her breath, and brushed the nasty arachnid away as silently as possible.

The men moved on, and she let out the breath she was

holding. Her chest hurt as air refilled her lungs, and tears of relief rolled down her cheeks.

Rowanne listened and waited. She heard nothing more but didn't risk moving for another half hour.

Were they gone for good or just searching farther into the woods and coming back her way?

Rowanne had no way of knowing. She crept out of her spot. Found a place to relieve herself, then crawled back into her tree. She closed her eyes and willed the men not to come back.

CHAPTER SIX

Monday, February 6th.

<u>Louisiana Forest</u>

Rowanne opened her eyes, and a chipmunk was sitting in the leaves in front of her tree, staring at her. She smiled. "You're a cutey. Can you spare me a nut? I'm starving."

He flicked his tail and scurried away at lightning speed, kicking up dried leaves behind him.

Silly as it was, she was sad to see him go. She liked the idea of having some company while she felt so lost and alone.

Stiff and sore from being scrunched up in such a small space, she crawled out over the roots and stood up. Breathing in the crisp morning air, Rowanne stretched her arms and legs and found a place farther into the trees to use as a bathroom.

She straightened her wrinkled clothes with her hand and patted down her wild hair. "Okay," she said to herself. "Today, I'll find a road and hitch a ride home."

With the sun rising in the east, she got her baring and started walking. She'd traveled through the trees and brush for about an hour before she heard a new sound—

running water.

Rowanne veered off her path to the right and found the creek. Shallow, only a few inches deep and a couple of feet wide but flowing fast. The water looked clean. She could see the stones, the silver minnows, and the soft brown soil on the creek bottom. Moisture dampened her knees as she dropped at the edge of the water, cupped her hands, and drank.

The water was ice-cold, and she felt it trickle all the way down to her empty belly. Shifting to kneel on a thick layer of pine needles, she opened her backpack and took out her empty water bottle. She filled it from the gurgling stream and put the cap on tight.

Back on track, she felt encouraged that she might make it. Where—she didn't know. Anywhere away from those men would work for her.

Horrible flashes of the man holding her down came into her head. She pushed the thoughts away and focused on other, more important memories: her mother, whom she missed every single day, her father, and how desperately she wanted him to be well again, her Great Gran, and all the fun they had catching frogs when she visited the bayou.

Police Headquarters, New Orleans

Luke met with Lieutenant White, head of missing persons, at nine a.m. He sat down in the only guest chair and waited for the update.

"Not much to report, Ranger Hyslop, but I guarantee

we've been doing everything in our power to find her."

"I believe you, sir. Thinking along a different line, let me ask you a couple of questions."

"Go ahead."

"How many other teenage girls have been reported missing in the past months or even year?"

"More than a few, I'm sure. Why do you ask?"

"It's not a situation I want to think of Rowanne being in, but we have to consider sex trafficking."

"What makes you think that's what we're dealing with?"

"Well, they use recruiters—young kids to befriend the girls and gain their confidence. We know Rowanne was intercepted at the local bus stop by a group of boys and taken from there. Then the girls are sold to handlers who run them at hotels, private residences, wherever they can gather customers. Casey and the girls scried for her and believed she was held along the water in the tourist hotel section."

"Do you have any proof of this?"

"No. It's all been through our spiritual side of investigating things. Now, my Gran is certain she sees Rowanne in the woods somewhere. Casey and I spent all yesterday tromping through every forest, glade, and grove in the area but don't have much to go on beyond Gran seeing trees."

"You think she's been moved again? By men using her for their gain."

Luke sighed. "I don't know, and I'm hoping against

it. My question to you is this, could you introduce me to your sex crimes squad and maybe help me get an inside track?"

It spoke to the man's character that the lieutenant didn't even hesitate. "Come, I'll take you upstairs and introduce you to the officers you'll need to speak with."

Luke rose, grateful for the help. "Thank you, lieutenant. I want to find out all I can."

Upstairs, Lieutenant White introduced Luke to Detectives Nan Scarlett and Brandy Kroll, two career police officers with stellar records specializing in violent sex crimes. He shook hands with them both, and they offered him a chair.

"Tell us about your niece, Ranger Hyslop," said Scarlett. "We do have some irons in the fire, and maybe we can work together."

"That's all I want," said Luke, "because if Rowanne is a victim, then there are other girls like her out there. I want to find them all and shut the operation down."

"And you have experience in violent crime?" asked Kroll.

"I'm on leave from the Blackmore Agency, the specialized Violent Crime Squad for the state of Texas."

Scarlett's brows lifted as she smiled. "I'm envious, Ranger Hyslop. I'd like to meet Ranger Blackmore. I've read some of his publications and he's brilliant."

"I'll be sure to bring Blaine in to meet y'all the next time he's in town."

That brought smiles to the girls' faces.

<u>Food Fantastic Magazine, New Orleans</u>

Misty waited outside the editor's office for her appointment. She'd arrived a little early, anxious to start her investigation into Leo's death. He'd said *pages* in his message. She understood that pages could mean anything, but it could also refer to the pages of his own magazine.

The editor's door opened, and a short lady with a platinum bob smiled at her and offered her hand. "Madam LeJeune, I'm Gisele Thibodeau. We can talk in my office."

Misty followed her into the bright, cheery office and sat down in one of the leather club chairs. Framed posters of many of New Orleans' famous restaurants lined the walls.

"Let me start by saying how devastated we all are by Leo's death. He'd been with us for years and was an integral part of our magazine family."

Misty appreciated the affection Gisele showed toward Leo and hoped it translated into her wanting to help find his killer. "Was there anyone here at the magazine who *didn't* like Leo?"

"Not that I know of. Leo was a sweet and genuine man. Always pleasant, eager to chat about the important events in everyone's life. We all loved him."

"It might be too soon to ask this question," said Misty, "but who is in line to take over Leo's column?"

Gisele's phone buzzed, but she sent it to voicemail. "No one has officially been assigned his column yet, but his assistant, Jamie Wolfe, will probably take over. He's familiar with Leo's methods and his style."

"And would it be possible for me to speak with Jamie for five minutes?"

"Jamie is on assignment this week out of the city. He won't be back for a few days at least."

"Oh, and when did he leave?"

"Early this morning."

Misty nodded. "One more question, if you don't mind. Do you keep a file of Leo's unfavorable reviews? From following his column, I realize you publish mostly the good ones, but have there ever been truly horrendous ones? How often do those come about?"

Gisele nodded. "A couple. And not often. More often than not, restaurants are deemed mediocre. When the food isn't bad but also isn't anything special, we don't bother publishing the reviews."

"And does that happen often?"

"It does. If there is nothing to write about and nothing interesting to tell our fans, those restaurants get left out."

Misty wondered if getting ignored was enough incentive to kill someone. She didn't think so but had no idea. For now, she'd focus on the bad reviews. "Did Leo give out any scathing reviews lately?"

"Are you thinking one of the restaurant owners could have killed him?"

"I don't know. I'm just trying to make sense of a senseless loss. Leo was a dear friend, and I want to see justice done."

Gisele fiddled with a stack of photographs on her desk. Her phone rang again, and again she sent the call to her inbox. "I can't remember any terrible reviews, and I'm sure I would have made note of the restaurant. Sorry. I must get back to work."

Misty stood. "Of course. I understand completely. Would it be possible for me to get copies of back issues for the past six months?"

"Certainly, Madam. I'll get Charlie to bundle them up for you." Gisele rose and walked Misty to her office door.

When her phone rang a third time, Misty turned and pointed back into her office. "Please, get that. I've taken enough of your time and can show myself out."

Gisele nodded and hustled back to her desk. "Let me know if you find anything. We're all so anxious to understand what happened to poor Leo."

On her way to the elevator, Misty paused and asked one of the girls to point out the cubicle for Leo's replacement.

"Jamie's not here today," she said.

Misty flashed the girl her best smile. "Gisele mentioned that. I'm sorry I missed him and wanted to leave a note."

The girl smiled. "Oh, sure, I'll show you." She walked to the other side of the room and pointed to an empty cubicle. "He sits there."

"Thank you." Misty waited until she was gone, then searched the desk for something that wouldn't be missed. She picked up a stress ball and a pair of discarded sunglasses with one arm missing.

Discretely, she shoved both items into her purse and floated across the room to the elevator.

Louisiana Forest

Rowanne tramped through the forest, the back of her heels chaffed and bleeding from her loose-fitting army boots. Picking a stable, moss-covered log, she sat down and pulled her feet free from their torture. She winced as the leather rubbed over the raw areas on both her heels.

Concentrating on examining the damage to her feet, she didn't hear the approach of the animal. A furry face touched her arm. She jumped, let out a little squeal, and the little brown and white hound dog scampered back a few yards.

"Oh, sorry, doggie," she said, pressing a hand on her racing heart. "I didn't mean to scare you."

She reached forward and sent out friendly, non-threatening vibes. "Are you hungry? Are you lost like me? We should try to find some food."

Rowanne unzipped her backpack and took out the water bottle. She gulped a couple of slurps of creek water, then gritted her teeth as she put her boots back on. "These boots are going to hurt with every step I take, doggie. Do you have a name?"

The dog wagged its tail.

She waited, hand outstretched until she trusted her enough to come close again. When she seemed relaxed, she patted her head and her long velvety ears. "I'll call you Nixa because you came to me from the west." She stared in the direction and screwed up her face. "At least, I think that way is west."

Nixa wagged her tail, and Rowanne took that as her new friend confirming it.

"I wish I had a biscuit for you." She laughed. "I wish I had a biscuit for me too. You wouldn't happen to know of any great take-out restaurants in this forest, would you?"

The dog canted its head as if trying to figure her out.

"Yeah, never mind. I wasn't really holding my breath."

Nine Saint Gillian Street

Luke had been back from the police station for about an hour before Misty came back from her errand with an armful of magazines. He greeted her in the front foyer and gave her a big hug. She was cold. Again. He needed to start making sure she was taking care of herself properly. When her mind got busy, Misty often lost track of the basic things in her life—like wearing a warm enough jacket.

"Let's relax in the sitting room with a cup of honey tea and compare notes. We're working on two different things, but we may be able to help each other."

"You can definitely help me," said Misty as she hung up her coat. "There's information I need, and I know you can get it for me."

Luke smiled. "Are you hot on the trail of Leo's

killer?"

"You bet I am." Misty led them into the kitchen and set the tray on the counter. While she boiled the kettle and poured them both a cup of restorative honey tea, he went over and grabbed the baking container by the stove.

With their haul in order, he carried everything into the sitting room across the hall.

"What have you got?" Misty asked, eyeing the container.

"Angelique made muffins while we were out." Luke picked one out of the container and took a bite. "I'm starving."

Once Misty selected her muffin, she sat deeper on the sofa and started to relax. "What did Lieutenant White have to say?"

"Not much, but I met two detectives that handle sex crimes. I have them looking for Rowanne, and they have her picture."

Misty's gaze held way too much sympathy for him to take. "You think a pimp or somebody like that has her?"

Luke nodded. "Unfortunately, that's where my instincts are taking me. The two detectives are working on tracking down several young girls that have been reported missing. They've been working on zeroing in on a sex trafficking ring in the city for a few months now. The problem is, they move so often, by the time they get a lead, the girls are gone."

Misty sipped at her tea. "I'm sorry, sugar. For Rowanne and Sam's sake as well as yours and your

Gran's, I hope you're wrong on this one."

Luke finished chewing his first muffin and started in on a second. "One thing I'm sure of, Rowanne will fight to get away from them. And that introduces two possible opposite results. Either she'll get away clean, or they'll catch her. Door number two likely means they beat her or kill her after they bring her back to wherever."

"Then we focus on door number one," said Misty.

He wished he could keep his mind there. "The detectives have several venues under surveillance, and they'll be in touch if they spot Rowanne."

"I'm glad more people are looking for her, sugar, and you and Casey left all those pictures at the hotels yesterday. Surely somebody will see a girl with flaming red hair."

Luke couldn't think about that anymore. "All right. Time to think of something else for a bit. What have you been up to?"

Misty dumped her purse on the sofa between them and showed him a stress ball and a pair of broken sunglasses. "These belong to the person who will take over Leo's column. He wasn't at his desk, and I borrowed a couple of items to see if I got any vibes."

"Borrowed?"

Misty giggled. "I'll give them back. I'm not cruel enough to steal a man's stress ball."

He set his tea back onto the tray and sat up. "Do you want to try them now?"

"No, I'm tired. Let's enjoy our time-out break, and

I'll try later upstairs in our room."

He loved that they'd progressed from your room and my room to 'our' room. He met her warm, emerald gaze and sent thanks up to the goddess for their budding relationship. He didn't know what kind of mess he'd be if he didn't have Misty's love and support behind him.

He brushed his fingers against her cheek and winked. "What did you want me to find for you, sweetheart?"

"Leo's protégé at the magazine is a man named Jamie Wolfe. I need his home address. He's out of town for the next few days on assignment, so there's a window of opportunity."

"Do you think he's Leo's killer?"

"I have no idea. Not yet, anyway."

Luke chuckled. "Well, you can't break into his house if you don't even know if he's a suspect."

"If I break into his house, then I have unlimited access to all his possessions, and I can be sure whether or not he's a suspect."

Luke gave her his sternest look. "Start with the possessions you already stole and have here. We can dig for another day or two. If Jamie Wolfe is out of town for a few days, you don't need to make any rash decisions."

Misty frowned. "Always the sensible one."

Luke leaned forward and kissed her pouting lips. "One of us has to be, Mist."

After their tea break, Misty grabbed the back issues of the magazines she brought home with her, and Luke went upstairs to work on the desk in his old room. The sex crime detectives had forwarded copies of a few case files, and he was eager to study them. Misty closed the door of the sitting room to shut out the noise of the house, retreated to the sofa, and called Craig. "Hey, there. How are you holding up, Craig?"

"Oh, getting by, Madam LeJeune."

Misty flipped through the first magazine and found Leo's column. "I spoke to Leo's editor this morning, and I wondered if he ever spoke about people at work, specifically anyone he wasn't getting along with?"

"Umm… could this wait until after the funeral, Madam? I'm sorry, I'm terribly distracted at the moment."

Is someone there with him?

Misty was reasonably sure she heard someone speaking in the background. "Of course, I'm sorry to have interrupted while you have company. Let's talk when you're alone."

"Oh, no," he said. "I'm quite alone. I simply have too many things on my mind, what with the preparations for the funeral and all."

"Do you need help with Leo's funeral?"

"That's kind of you, Madam, but I'd rather take care of it on my own."

"And what's the name of the funeral home y'all are using?"

"Leo is resting at Serenity Gardens. They have a website with directions."

"Thank you."

Misty hung up and frowned at her cellphone. She must be mistaken about someone in the background speaking with Craig because why would he lie?

Misty put Craig out of her mind for the moment and sorted through a few more of the magazines. Leo's bio picture at the top of his columns made her smile. He'd been such a sweet man and an excellent writer. He could describe the succulence of a dish and make your mouth water.

After reading a few of his latest reviews, her heart grew heavy for the loss of a friend, and she set the magazines aside.

To cheer herself up, she headed upstairs to see how busy her mother was with the students. The energy of the girls was like a direct line to enthusiasm and happiness— like the most exceptional happy drug on the market.

She had to admit, she'd become addicted to them.

The students of their little witch school greeted her with smiles. "What are y'all working on today?"

Her mother waved her in. "We were talking this morning about mediums and channeling. I told the girls about going to Leo's house and what we learned. There was so much residual energy in that place, and I could have spent days in there."

Misty had felt it too. "Leo's house definitely has things to tell us. Maybe after the funeral, Craig will allow us to spend more time there. In the meantime, I have another school trip in mind, if all y'all can join me for a couple of hours."

Her mother smiled at her and then addressed the four students. "What say you about a school trip, children?"

Misty raised a finger. "And wait, there's more. I'll also include lunch along the way."

Diana clapped. "Fun. Whatever it is, I'm in."

"What did you have in mind, dear?" asked Claire.

Misty held up the note with the address of the funeral home. "I was thinking we'd go to the funeral home, take Daddy and see if Leo had anything else to tell us?"

Charlotte squealed and jumped to her feet. "Oh, talking to the dead. I *so* want to do that."

Casey nodded. "Yep, I'm in."

Misty looked at Michele. "Is it unanimous?"

Michele didn't look convinced. "Dead people make me nervous. I want to come, but I also don't."

Charlotte patted her arm. "There's nothing to be afraid of. We'll all be there, right?"

"Right," said Casey with a grin. "I'll protect y'all from any half-crazed spirits that haven't crossed over."

Michele shivered. "I'm a bit freaked out by the concept, but I'm in. I don't want to be the only one missing out on the fun."

"Attagirl," said Misty.

Everyone gathered in the foyer while Misty told Luke where they were going. "Do you want to come with, sugar?"

"No. I'll wait for any phone calls about Rowanne and work on the other angle. Gran isn't feeling well today, and

I don't want to be too far away in case she needs me. Angelique is making her some soup."

Misty gave Luke a quick kiss goodbye and patted Hoo on the head. They all trudged out through the back garden to the Expedition parked at the back gate.

A sudden wave of nausea sweep over her as Misty slid behind the wheel. With the hustle of everyone piling in, no one seemed to notice. Her mother rode in the passenger seat, Casey and the three girls in two rows behind.

Misty lowered her window and welcomed the cool breeze on her face as she drove down the lane. Better. That was much better.

Tulane-Gravier District, New Orleans

Serenity Gardens was situated in a vast old Victorian on a quiet street where each property boasted mature trees and sprawling green lawns. The owners had restored the house beautifully and turned it into a showplace.

Misty parked the truck around back in the designated area and led the way in the side door with her entourage.

A tall man in a somber gray suit greeted them in a thickly carpeted entranceway. "Hello. Welcome to Serenity Gardens. We have no viewings until two p.m. this afternoon."

Misty dipped her chin and smiled. "I realize that sir, but we desperately need a moment alone with my dear friend, Leo Pinoit. I am missing him terribly. Would you mind if we had a few moments of privacy so the girls could say their goodbyes?"

She handed the man one of the embossed black cards she rarely parted with. With no need and no desire to advertise, she scolded herself for having them printed in the first place.

His eyes widened as he stared at the card for a moment before finding his voice. "Aw, Madam LeJeune. It's wonderful to meet you in person. Of course, I'll show you where Mr. Pinoit is resting and ensure you won't be disturbed."

Misty squeezed his arm. "Thank you so much."

He escorted them down the hall and into one of the more spacious viewing rooms. Perhaps Leo would be drawing a large crowd at two o'clock.

Banks of floral tributes had already arrived, and Leo's room was adorned on three sides by lush bouquets of lilies, roses, carnations, and many other flowers Misty didn't recognize. Her expertise was in the healing flowers, herbs, and roots.

The air in the room hung heavily perfumed. It was almost overpowering, considering how nauseous she'd felt earlier.

Misty moved closer and gazed down at Leo resting in his coffin. Dressed in a dark pin-striped designer suit, he looked a bit like an undertaker himself. "Looking good, Leo. Daddy's here if you feel like talking."

Josiah manifested in his usual greenish silver glow. He stood close to the end of the coffin, and the girls sucked in a breath and took a step back.

"Can y'all see Daddy?" asked Misty in a whisper.

"This is the first time I've seen him," said Charlotte. "So exciting."

"Isn't it?" Claire moved closer to Josiah and said, "Talk to him, Josiah. We haven't got much private time here."

"All right, dear."

Everyone stood around the coffin in a silent semi-circle and listened. The sounds on the air weren't human, and Claire strained to make out what her dead husband was saying to the recently departed, Leo.

Then an eerie monotone filled the airwaves.

"Don't look for the wolf in the forest when it's sitting in your backyard."

Michele clamped her hand over her mouth to keep from screaming, and Diana held tight to Casey's hand.

"I see Monsieur LeJeune and heard a dead man speak." Charlotte pegged the others, her excitement palpable. "This is the best day of my life."

Misty giggled. "Perhaps we'll save the celebration until after we leave the funeral home. Somber faces, everyone."

Popeye's

At lunch on the way home from the funeral home, all the talk was about Leo and what he said. "It would be far easier," said Claire, "if Leo refrained from being so cryptic and came out and told us who killed him."

Misty set her soda down and smiled. "Maybe he doesn't know, or only has suspicions."

Casey accepted the leftover fries that Diana didn't want and nodded. "People only eat at restaurants, at a friend's house, or at home. Leo was on his way to the restaurant to have dinner with Misty and Luke, so it stands to reason that the poisoned food he ate was at home. His lunch, or maybe an afternoon snack before getting ready to go out."

Diana frowned. "But if you're eating at your own house, it wouldn't be poisoned. Misty said Leo was a great cook."

"Maybe somebody brought something to the house or cooked for him. You know, like Angelique."

Misty wondered about that. "That implies someone he welcomes into his home. Angelique doesn't stop by and give random people muffins. She cooks for her family and friends."

Charlotte nodded. "Right. Leo was already poisoned once. It makes sense that he'd be careful what he ate and who gave it to him. That might be what he meant by the wolf sitting in his backyard. It was someone he had no reason to suspect, maybe someone he ate or drank with before."

Misty wiped her fingers and nodded. "All sound reasoning. So the wolf was someone close to Leo— someone he trusted—then we need to make a shortlist and have Luke check into their backgrounds."

"I've never solved a murder before," said Michele.

"My guardian is a criminologist," said Casey to Michele. "I worked on background information in a lot of his cases."

Misty nodded. "I forgot that, sweetheart. You can work on our list. Lukey is consumed with finding Rowanne at the moment and has his hands full."

Nine Saint Gillian Street

After dinner, Luke retired to the sitting room with Misty and a flavored coffee. The house was quiet, and she wanted to spend some time focused on Jamie Wolfe's red stress ball and his broken sunglasses.

"Which one do you want to try first?" he asked.

"He probably handled the ball a lot more. I'll start there." Misty picked up the ball and held it gently in her right hand. She closed her eyes, and they waited for Jamie Wolfe's energy to come to her. After a minute or two, she began rambling in that low psychic voice that Luke found so unsettling.

Why is Leo inviting me to his house for dinner?

I'll offer to bring the wine.

Why does Leo put up with Craig?

When Misty opened her eyes, Luke handed her a glass of water. "Do you think the wine was poisoned?"

"I don't know."

"The lab work would show the contents of his stomach and how long it had been since he ate. I'll see if I can get a copy of the autopsy report from homicide." He pointed to the broken Ray-Bans. "You look exhausted, sweetheart. Leave those until tomorrow."

Misty stood up and stretched. "I felt a little sick and woozy a couple of times today. I need to go to bed early."

"Fine with me."

Misty giggled. "You're easy."

Luke winked as he pulled Misty close and kissed her with all the passionate love he felt for her. "Where you're concerned, I'm a pushover. I love you beyond reason."

Louisiana Forest

Another night alone in the forest was not her first choice, but since Rowanne had no choice—she searched for a relatively safe place for her and Nixa to hunker down and spend the night.

Darkness and the temperature were falling quickly, and she had to hurry. When nothing secure turned up, the best she could do was crawl under a huge evergreen. When she settled with Nixa close to the trunk of the massive tree, the heavy lower boughs covered them completely. No one walking by would see them, and the branches broke the wind and gave them a bit of a break from the cold—a bit.

Rowanne laid down with her head on her backpack and pulled Nixa close to her for warmth.

Nixa whined, and Rowanne heard the little dog's stomach growl. "I know, girl. You're hungry and so am I. Tomorrow we'll find some food. We have to."

She tuned out the scary night sounds of the forest and closed her eyes.

CHAPTER SEVEN

Tuesday, February 7th.

<u>Louisiana Forest</u>

Rowanne woke at daylight, more aware than ever of how desperately hungry she was. Her stomach growled, and she felt sick from being so empty. She thought of all the times her great gran had tried to make her eat oatmeal porridge.

"I want porridge right now, Gran," she said aloud, and Nixa wagged her tail. "With milk and brown sugar."

Thoughts of her sick father and how worried he must be caused tears to burn behind her eyes. She blinked quickly and fought them off.

"Why didn't I think of how much I'd hurt him and Uncle Luke and Gran when I ran away?" She picked up her backpack and struggled with the straps. "I've been mean and selfish and so busy thinking I'm better than everyone, I ruined everything. Casey was right when he called me a bitch. And Claire was right too. I have to do better and get rid of all my negativity if I want my powers to work."

Rowanne winced as she shoved bare feet into her

boots. "I wish I had a pair of big, puffy socks."

I wish I had a lot of things.

"Come on, Nixa, we'll starve if we sit here wishing for food. We have to get going and find some."

Nixa jumped up, ready to go.

"I'm glad I have you." Rowanne leaned down and patted her head. "Despite everything I said. I don't like being alone."

Nine Saint Gillian Street

Gran was in her room, getting dressed when images of Rowanne flashed through her head. All she saw were the trees again—nothing but trees, but she heard Rowanne talking to someone and saying how hungry she was.

Gran blinked back tears and went downstairs to tell Luke. She held tight to the hand railing, putting one foot in front of the other.

Misty crossed the kitchen, intending to pour herself a cup of tea. The smell of eggs cooking on the stove hit her, and her stomach flipped. As her gag reflex triggered, she bolted into the powder room and dropped before the porcelain toilet.

With nothing much in her stomach, there wasn't much to throw up. She washed up, splashed some cold water on her face, and figured she was coming down with a flu of some sort.

I'll have to whip up an echinacea remedy.

When she came out of the bathroom, Luke was there leaning on the wall in the hallway. "Are you okay, sweetheart?"

She waved away the concern and smiled at him. "The smell of the eggs made me sick for some reason. Nothing to worry about. I'll have one of Angelique's muffins instead."

"That's it? You're not concerned?"

She smiled up at him but didn't understand the sudden panic in his face. "Concerned about what, sugar?"

"Think about it," said Luke. "You haven't been your usual bundle of endless energy, you were woozy yesterday, and now you're throwing up first thing in the morning."

Misty's eyes widened. "No. You don't think…"

"Could you be?"

She thought about it and shrugged. "I guess I could be. But it's so soon. We're just working out our rhythm as a couple. And you… starting a family must bring up a lot of heartaches." Her eyes stung as she thought about Luke's dead wife and little girl. "I'm sorry. I didn't mean for this to happen."

Luke pulled her against his chest and squeezed her tight. He held her a long time, and she listened to the strong and steady beat of his heart against her ear.

After her own heart slowed, he kissed the top of her head, pulled back, and meet her gaze head-on. "A baby is unexpected, yes, but if it's true, nothing would make me happier."

Misty's mind was spinning. A baby?

She didn't need to think about it anymore than that. She smiled at him. "I hope it is true. I've wanted a baby for a long time, and I would love for you to be the daddy."

Luke hugged her once more and placed a gentle palm against her belly. "Let's not get ahead of ourselves. We'll get you checked out at a clinic before we start making plans. Maybe you're right. Maybe it's a touch of the flu and an aversion to eggs."

Misty heard the caution in Luke's voice. She wished she knew if his worry stemmed from whether she *was* pregnant or whether she *wasn't*. Well, time would tell.

When they returned to the kitchen, her mother was seated next to Luke's Gran and was comforting her.

"What is it, Gran?" he said, closing the distance between them.

"I had another message from Rowanne."

Luke sat down beside his grandmother and held her hand. "What did she say, Gran? Is she okay?"

Tears welled in Gran's tired old eyes. "All I could see were trees, Lukey, but Rowanne is hungry. So hungry, she said she'd eat my porridge." Gran shook her white head. "And she always hated porridge when I made it for her."

Luke nodded. "She's somewhere in the woods with no food, and she might not have warm clothes or any shelter. We have to find her soon."

Louisiana Forest

Rowanne trudged forward for another two or three hours

hoping to find something. A road, a house, a store, a camper. Some hint of civilization with a promise of help. Nixa ran alongside her, chasing the odd squirrel or chipmunk, and once the little hound dog ran under a bush and scared up a bird.

Rowanne screamed when the bird flew out the leaves and almost right into her. "Don't do that, puppy. You scared me."

Nixa wagged her tail and ran on ahead.

For the past two days, the forest had looked the same on all sides—trees, bushes, fallen logs, leaves, and needles underfoot. Rowanne fought her way through the underbrush, certain that anything ahead was better than what lay behind her.

The trees grew close together, and she pushed branches and limbs out of her way. Her arms and legs were scratched and red, and she had nothing to put on them to soothe the stinging.

Then when she was convinced the forest would go on forever, the trees thinned slightly, and more sun shone through. She hadn't realized she was walking downhill, but the trees eventually gave way, and the traveling got easier.

After another half an hour, a tiny wooden building appeared in a small clearing. What was it? A hunting shack? There was no road access or any easy way to get there. A ranger's cabin? Did New Orleans have forest rangers?

Well, if it was a ranger's cabin, there would be a radio.

Nixa ran to the door and whined. Rowanne tried the knob, and it turned. They went inside, and she closed the door behind them. The place was tiny. A narrow cot sat against one wall, and the opposite wall held a couple of shelves holding four tins of food—two cans of beans and two cans of stew.

Rowanne walked over to the shelf and examined the tins. "Food, Nixa. Can you believe it?"

Nixa followed her across the room and sat next to her leg as she searched for a can opener. She hadn't seen it at first because it was hanging on a nail on the wall. Rowanne opened the tin, picked up the only spoon she saw and wiped it clean on her t-shirt. She ate cold stew out of the can and wondered when anything had tasted so good.

Nixa whined, and Rowanne felt sorry for her. She scooped a glob of stew out of the tin onto the dirty wooden floor, and Nixa gobbled it up. Feeling guilty for not giving her more, she gave her another pile.

After they ate, Rowanne plopped on the cot and pulled off her boots. Her heels were bleeding, and she ignored the pain, so thankful for a place to rest. She lay down on the cot and pulled up the thin blanket.

Nine Saint Gillian Street

Witch classes were cancelled for the day because of Leo's funeral. The girls and Casey were attending as observers and hoping to get vibes from any of Leo's so-called friends or co-workers that came to pay their respects. Many of the mourners who loved Leo would be genuinely grieving, but some who didn't love him as much would be putting up a false front.

Sorting out the truly bereaved from the curious or the nosy was their assignment. That and assessing the eight people Casey came up with on the suspect shortlist, personal assistant Craig, younger brother, Tony, protégé Jamie, editor Gisele, housekeeper Muriel, professional rival, William, and friendly neighbors Greg and Antoine.

Surely her fledgling witches would get positive or negative vibes as they came in close contact with those who knew Leo.

Misty was sure that one person at the funeral would be Leo's murderer. They had to discern which one.

Tulane-Gravier District, New Orleans

The chapel inside Serenity Gardens was packed to capacity when Luke, Misty, Claire, and the students arrived for the service. Leo Pinoit was a celebrity of sorts and a hero to the gourmets and foodies in the state who dedicated themselves to finding the best food and the best service Louisiana had to offer.

Luke hadn't anticipated the media turnout, and the gridlock the vans caused in the vicinity of the funeral home. Reporters and camera people roamed the sidewalk in front of the Serenity property, waiting for an opportunity to catch a moment for the news at six. He didn't want them filming Misty.

She's an even bigger celebrity in this city than Leo.

Most of the pews were full, and sitting together

wasn't an option. Casey found a spot for Diana and himself, Charlotte and Michele squeezed in at the end of a row, and Luke found a spot near the back of the chapel big enough for Misty and Claire.

"I'll stand at the back and watch," he whispered to Misty as she sat down.

Long and tearful, the pastor's portion of the service was punctuated by kind words from many representatives from the booming New Orleans restaurant community. After Leo's favorite psalm, the service ended with a moving eulogy given by Leo's younger brother, Tony Pinoit.

After one more hymn and a final prayer, the minister invited everyone to join the procession to the gravesite, and then back to Leo's townhome for coffee and cake.

Louisiana Forest

A noise outside the cabin woke Rowanne, and a surge of fear ripped through her. Were the men there to retake her prisoner? She scrambled to get to her feet and stopped short. Staring down at her was the handsome face of a boy about her age.

She blinked and looked again. His clothes were ragged and seemed too small for him, and his brown hair was long, tangled, and decorated with leaves and twigs. The rat's nest hung in curly ringlets around his neck.

He peered at her with big brown eyes and didn't speak.

Rowanne felt she was under a microscope the way the

boy examined her from head to toe. "Hi, sorry. I... um, didn't know this was your place."

"Why are you on my bed?"

"Is this your house?" asked Rowanne.

"I found it first."

"I didn't know. Sorry. Okay, I should tell you, I ate one of your tins of food."

"You'll have to pay me back."

Rowanne's heart raced. What did he mean by that? After what happened to her, she wouldn't let anyone force her to do anything ever again. "I don't have anything for you."

"I'll think of something." He squatted down, so he was at eye level with her. "What's your name?"

"Rowanne." She sat up, lifted her backpack off the floor, and rifled through the contents for her smokes. She found her lighter and put a Tijuana in her mouth.

"Don't smoke in my house."

Rowanne got to her feet. "I'll go outside. Come on, Nixa."

"That's not a dog name," he said. "Where did you get him?"

"Her," said Rowanne. She tramped outside, and the boy followed. "Nixa found me lost in the forest."

Rowanne kept walking until she found a stump close to the shack and sat down. She lit up her smoke and tried to relax. Hard to do with a boy standing in front of her, staring, and watching her smoke.

"You didn't tell me your name," she said.

"Don't have one."

"How can you not have a name?" asked Rowanne.

He shrugged. "I woke up here one day. That's the first I remember."

"I'm not calling you a liar, but that doesn't sound true. What should I call you if you don't have a name?"

"You could give me a name."

Rowanne smiled. "You remind me of Pan."

He shook his head. "I don't like it. It makes me sound like a skillet or a pot to cook in."

Rowanne laughed. "Not that kind of a pan. Let me think of something better. Umm, how about Ben?"

"Okay, Ben is good."

Rowanne giggled.

"Your hair is red."

"Your eyesight is good."

"Never seen a girl with hair that red color."

Rowanne took a big drag and blew out the smoke. "Now, you have." She looked him up and down and decided he was much too thin for his height. "How long have you lived here in this little shack?"

"Long time."

"Days? Weeks? Years?"

"Yep."

"Which one?"

"Can't remember."

"Is there a road near here, or a store or a house or something? I need to use a phone."

"Didn't see any."

"How did you get here? You must have come from somewhere close by?"

"Don't think so."

"You just woke up one day in the middle of the forest?"

"Pretty much." Ben took a step closer to her.

"I'm a witch."

"Lie. There are no witches."

"I'm not a liar, Ben. Sometimes my spells work perfectly if there's enough positive energy around me."

Ben sat down on the ground and trained his brown, puppy dog eyes on her. "Show me something you can do. Do one of your tricks."

"I don't do tricks. I do magick."

"Magick isn't real. I don't believe you."

"What do you believe? How do you survive out here? What do you eat?"

"I hunt for food with my bow and arrow and cook it over a fire."

"I didn't see any bow in the shack."

"I hide it, in case strangers come." He pointed. "Like you. You're a stranger, and I can't trust you."

"You can trust me," said Rowanne. "I won't do anything to hurt you."

Ben smiled for the first time, and it warmed her heart

for reasons unknown. "Don't do witch stuff when I'm not looking and put a hex on me."

"Don't do anything to hurt me or piss me off, and I won't."

He laughed. "I like you. You're kind of funny."

"I'm not feeling too funny right now. I'm lost and hungry, and I need to call my uncle."

Crescent Cemetery, Marigny

Misty held Luke's hand as they walked towards Leo's freshly dug grave. A cold drizzle had begun to fall, and the chill of it was sinking into her bones. Luke was worried. She felt it bleeding off him in waves and saw it in his eyes every time he looked at her. He'd been watching her since their conversation about pregnancy earlier that day. He was happy with the idea but terrified too.

She understood his fear. He'd already lost his wife and child. She doubted he would survive losing another. If she was pregnant, he would guard her and their child with his life. He would fight to never let anything happen to them.

Her mother opened a big, black umbrella, and Misty crowded underneath. "Let's see if Daddy notices anything at the gravesite. He's dynamite in cemeteries and funeral homes."

"Thank you, child," her father said. "It's good to know I'm still dynamite in one area, at least."

Claire giggled at her dead husband.

Misty rolled her eyes.

The crowd of mourners assembled around the open grave was large and growing larger as they approached. Misty wanted to touch the casket one more time to see if Leo might reach out to her. His spirit should be incensed at being eliminated before the Fates had destined his time to depart. Leo should be shouting at the top of his dead lungs for justice.

"I need to get closer," she whispered to Luke.

"Casey, take Misty's arm on that side and protect her from the crowd. We have to get closer."

Casey let go of Diana and helped clear a path for Misty to reach the coffin.

"Gather closer, friends, and relatives." The minister began the interment service with a long prayer, and Misty had to put her plan on hold for a few minutes. While she waited for an opportunity, she focused on the crowd and blinked twice when she saw Leo manifest himself above the head of Gisele Thibodeau, the magazine editor.

Misty turned to Claire and whispered, "See that, Mother?"

"Yes, I do. Who is that woman?"

"His boss, the editor of the food magazine."

"Leo is telling us something," said Claire. "He's singling her out for a reason."

Marigny District, New Orleans

Craig, with the help of a catering company and her staff, hosted the funeral reception in Leo's townhome and put on a lavish display of food and wine.

Misty wondered if Craig had any right to stay on in Leo's house if his employer was deceased. Was the house being left to Craig in Leo's will? Could that be a motive for murder?

Right. The will. *I need a copy of the will.*

Misty expressed her sadness to Tony Pinoit, Leo's younger brother. Although she'd never met him in person, Leo had mentioned him many times in his private sessions.

"Madam LeJeune, Leo spoke of you often and how helpful you were guiding him along life's path. I'd love to come myself and have a reading in the near future."

"Please do, and the sooner, the better. I'm interested in discussing several things that are troubling me about your brother's death."

Tony raised an eyebrow. A handsome man, Tony must have been at least fifteen years younger than Leo. "Troubling, Madam LeJeune? Could you give me a hint about what you'd like to discuss?"

"Not here and not today, but there are matters Leo and I feel are pressing."

Tony inhaled quickly. "Have you been in touch with Leo since…?"

"Yes, I have."

Tony's interest seemed intensified. "Perhaps I could stop by tomorrow."

Misty nodded. "That would be wonderful."

Louisiana Forest

Rowanne pretended not to watch Ben go into the cabin to retrieve his bow from its secret hiding place. Not so secret anymore. The cot was the only piece of furniture in the shack, so the only logical place to hide it would be under the cot.

Still, she wouldn't ruin his illusion of stealth.

Especially because, with a handful of homemade arrows, he left her smoking on her stump and tramped off into the woods looking for their dinner.

May the goddess be with you on your hunt.

Rowanne stroked Nixa's head. "How long has that kid lived out here all alone?"

Nixa wagged her tail and didn't share the answer.

Ben was gone for almost two hours, and Rowanne worried he wouldn't be back before dark. She was on her feet, ready to go looking for him when she heard a twig snap.

She froze and ducked into the shadow of the cabin.

Nixa barked a couple of times and ran towards the noise.

Wearing a big smile on his dirty sweat-smeared face, Ben burst through the trees, a dead rabbit dangling from his belt.

Rowanne made a face at the sight of the dead animal, and Ben pointed a finger at her. "You'll be happy to eat a rabbit if you get hungry enough, red-haired girl."

"I am hungry, and so is Nixa."

Rowanne couldn't bear to watch as Ben skinned the rabbit and gutted it. She busied herself gathering wood while Ben got the meat ready, then she helped him build a fire in the circle of stones in front of the shack.

He sat on the ground, skillfully using his knife and fashioned a sturdy spit out of sticks. He sharpened the end of another stick, skewered the rabbit and set the skewer in place on the spit, low enough over the fire to roast the meat.

Rowanne observed everything in case she ever had to cook outside by herself. She might have to if no one ever found her, and she was here forever like Ben.

Ben is smart in a slow kind of way.

After dividing the rabbit between them and eating almost all of it, Ben gave the leftovers to the dog. Nixa happily chomped down everything she was given and looked for more.

It was full dark by the time they finished eating. Ben tossed handfuls of dirt on the fire to put it out before heading inside the little shack.

"I go to bed after I eat because it's dark, and there's nothing else to do until daylight."

"That's okay," said Rowanne. "I'm tired too. I had a couple of horrible days. Worst ever in my life."

"Want to tell me what happened to you? People don't hide in the woods because they like the smell of trees."

Not sure whether she should tell him or not, Rowanne began slowly, telling Ben what happened since she stupidly decided to run away from Nine Saint Gillian

Street.

Ben listened to the whole sordid tale without interrupting until she finished. "Do you think the bad men will keep looking for you?"

"I hope they gave up," said Rowanne, "but they were mean people, and I saw their faces. I can identify them to the police. They might want me dead."

"We shouldn't let our guard down. If they haven't given up, we should be prepared."

"I don't want you to be in danger because of me. It's not your problem. You have a quiet life here, although I can't figure out why you're here in the first place."

"Good question, red-haired girl. Like I said before, I don't know the answer."

Rowanne didn't know what to think about that. "Huh, I guess it's a mystery then, isn't it?"

"Guess so."

Sitting on the side of the cot, Rowanne pulled a candle from her backpack and set it on the floor. "Watch."

Candle wax
With smoke and fire
Ignite, I beg you
Flame burn higher
So mote it be.

Rowanne chanted the spell and pointed her intension at the candle. *Poof.* The wick lit and the candle burned brightly.

Ben's eyes blinked wide as a genuine smile broke across his dirty face. "Wow, good one. I thought you were bullshitting me on the witch thing."

"Nope. I have powers, and I'm training them, but I'm still learning. I go to a school for witches that my Uncle Luke's girlfriend runs at her house."

"Can I go there? I never got to go to school."

"If we ever get to N'Orlean, I'll make sure you can go to my school."

"Thanks. You won't forget, will you?"

"Nope. I won't forget. I owe you a lot already, and I have to pay you back for eating your stew, remember?"

"Time to sleep." Ben kicked off his raggedy boots and laid down on the cot in his filthy clothes. "Come on. We've got one little bed. You have to squeeze in here beside me."

Rowanne wondered about getting close to Ben, but her only other option was lying on the floor with no mattress and no blanket.

She tugged off her boots, wincing at the soreness of her unhealed blisters. She cuddled in beside Ben and inhaled the sweaty musky smell of him. He smelled like boy and smoke and trees and leaves and something else she couldn't put her finger on.

It didn't matter.

All that mattered to her was that for the first night in three, she was warm, and for the moment, she felt safe. She could deal with everything else.

Rowanne closed her eyes and fell fast asleep.

CHAPTER EIGHT

Wednesday, February 8th.

Wednesday, February 8th.

<u>Louisiana Forest</u>

Rowanne was dreaming a good dream about her Daddy buying her a car. He was so happy she was home safe and vowed to be a better person, that he'd forgiven her all her past behavior and stupid mistakes. Her car was dark blue and had a silver design on the side. She woke with a start when Ben tugged her arm.

"We have to go," he whispered, a finger pressed to his lips. He pulled her up off the cot and propelled her out a back door she didn't know existed.

The woods were pitch dark, and Ben ran through the trees like a gazelle, holding her hand and pulling her forward at a pace so quick she imagined she was flying.

With no time to grab her boots, she was barefoot, and the leaves, pine needles, and twigs underfoot prickled her feet as she ran. Nixa was running alongside them, undetectable to her, except for the breathy panting by her feet.

Knowing her little dog was beside her gave her comfort.

Ben didn't slow down for a minute and allowed her no rest. Rowanne gasped for breath, her lungs aching inside her chest as she ran and ran. How far had they come? It became harder to breathe and harder to keep up.

Were they running uphill?

Ben slipped an arm around her waist and pull her tight to his body seconds before they flew through the air, terrifyingly weightless for a few seconds.

With an icy splash, they hit icy water.

Rowanne wanted to scream with every fiber of her being as they sank to the bottom of the lake or pond or whatever it was. She held her breath and felt Ben swimming. He was strong. So much stronger than he looked. He kicked and paddled with his one free arm and pulled her up to the surface.

With her head above water, he swam and pulled her along beside him. She would never have believed he was that strong.

She choked and spat water as he tossed her onto the bank and rolled her onto land. Grass. She felt it under her, touched it with her fingers, and inhaled the scent of it. Grass.

Ben held her close to his soaking wet body and rocked her. "Breathe. You're okay, little red-haired girl. Breathe in and out. They can't catch us now."

Rowanne lay still in his arms for a long time before she was able to speak. "Where are we?"

"In the park."

"A park?"

"Like a state park where nobody lives, and no campers are allowed."

"Like a wildlife preserve?"

"Maybe. Come on. I'll build a fire and dry us out. Can you walk a little way?"

Rowanne stood and tested her legs. Wobbly, but good enough. No boots. "How do you know which way to go?"

"I've been here a couple of times before. This part of the park is closer to a road. I've seen it."

Rowanne's heart thumped, thinking they might find help. "Like a paved road?"

"Not paved. Dirt." Ben tugged her along until he was happy with their spot. "We're safe here, but we don't have a good house like we had before."

"Maybe we can find another shack." Rowanne shivered in her wet clothes as she sat on a log and waited until Ben picked up twigs and leaves and piled them in a heap.

"My matches are in the shack. Can you light the fire?"

"I can try."

> *Goddess of fire*
> *Hear my desire*
> *Leaves, twigs, and sticks ignite*
> *Fire burning warm and bright*
> *So mote it be.*

Rowanne concentrated and chanted her spell three times before the little pile of kindling burst into flame.

Ben fanned the flame and got the blaze burning higher. "You're good at the fire thing, red-haired girl. Maybe you are a real witch."

"I like to think I am."

"I want to learn," said Ben. "I need to know things."

Nine Saint Gillian Street, New Orleans

Before dawn, Misty tore out of bed and ran into the ensuite. She knelt in front of the toilet and threw up everything in her stomach.

Luke came barreling into the bathroom and sat on the cold tile floor beside her. "Can I get you anything?"

"Mother told me to eat a couple of crackers."

"You told her?"

"I told her it was a *maybe,* and she got very excited for us."

"I guess we should make sure it's even a thing before everyone gets too excited."

Misty tried to smile. "First, the crackers."

Luke chuckled and kissed her head. "I'll grab my jeans and go down right now."

"Thanks."

Louisiana Forest

Ben was up at dawn, cutting branches off trees with his knife and laying them on the ground. Rowanne didn't have a clue what he was doing, but she admired his know-how and his ambition.

She crawled out from under the tree where they'd slept wishing for one of her smokes. "Can I help you do something?"

"I'm okay. It won't take me long. I want you to have a place to sit while I run back to the shack and get our stuff. It's going to rain."

Rowanne looked up at the blue sky and wondered if he was right. It didn't look like rain. "I should've cast a ward around the shack to protect us. I didn't think of it, I'm sorry. If you want to go back there, I can cast a protection spell over you."

Ben stopped chopping long enough to stare at her. "You saying you could have made the shack so they couldn't get us?"

"Not for sure. What I'm saying is—I should have tried."

"But what if you tried and it didn't work?"

"Then, we'd have to run again."

"Do you just say words, or do you need magick stuff?"

"I need things from nature to help me. Castor beans or salt or I could use rabbit feet. You must have a lot of those by now."

"I saved them in a hollow log."

"I saw you put them there," said Rowanne. "Rabbit's feet are lucky. We could use those."

"Do you want to risk going back there?" asked Ben.

"It's your home, and I don't feel right making you leave your home because of me. I'm saying we could make it more secure and make weapons to defend ourselves."

"You're a brave girl with red hair. I don't want to give up my home, but I don't want you to get taken by the bad men either. You were sent to me for a reason."

"Thank you, Ben. Do you think we could find another home if we walked down the dirt road?"

"Maybe. I never tried."

"While you're making whatever it is you're making, think about what you want to do, and I'll go along with whatever you decide."

Ben finished the lean-to and set the shelter up between two sturdy trees. "Stay in there until I come back. I'm going to get our stuff."

"I don't think you can carry it all," said Rowanne. "Do you have to swim across the lake?"

Ben chuckled. "No. No swimming. I'll go around. It takes longer, but I know the way, and I'm very fast."

Yes, he was. Unbelievably fast.

"Okay, good. I'll see you soon."

Nine Saint Gillian Street

Leo's younger brother, Tony, arrived shortly before nine-thirty. Angelique greeted him in the foyer, took his coat, and hung it in the front hall closet.

Misty pulled herself together sufficiently to speak to him in the parlor, but Luke insisted on being present in case anything untoward happened. She might get sick again, and he wasn't taking any chances.

"Please sit down, Tony," said Misty. "Angelique will make us some tea."

Dressed casually in black slacks and a tan cashmere sweater, Tony chose a chair on the opposite side of the table. Instead of settling in and relaxing, he perched on the edge of his seat and leaned towards the table.

Misty watched him run his hand through his dark hair—and again. Fidgety and tense, he couldn't seem to get comfortable.

"Did Leo speak to you about any trouble he was having with other employees at the magazine?" she asked.

"His boss, Gisele Thibodeau, gave him plenty of trouble. Almost every day, she called him into her office and made none too subtle overtures. She wanted things to be different between them and made no bones about her desire to be more than friends."

"But Leo wasn't interested in pursuing a relationship with her?"

"No," said Tony. "He was interested in someone else, who also worked at the magazine, but he never mentioned her name to me."

Misty raised an eyebrow. "That's interesting because when I saw him on New Year's Day, it came through in his reading that someone at his workplace was interested in him on a personal level. At the time, I didn't see who it was."

Angelique brought in a tea tray and placed it in the center of the round pedestal table. Misty poured three cups and passed the glass milk pitcher to Tony.

Luke pushed his tea to one side and made room to open his laptop. "A copy of your brother's autopsy report was sent to me this morning. The part I find most interesting is that the poison was in the wine, just as Misty suspected."

"But Jamie brought the wine," said Misty, "and I don't think Jamie had a motive to kill Leo."

"Do you know that, Madam LeJeune?" asked Tony.

"In a vision, I saw Jamie Wolfe standing at Leo's door with a bottle of wine in his hand. He wasn't thrilled to be there, but to me, he didn't seem possessed with murderous intent."

"Jamie Wolfe was next in line to take Leo's column," said Tony. "He'd be a feature writer instead of a contributor. Do you think he might have wanted the position badly enough to kill my brother to get it?"

"I don't," said Misty.

"We haven't ruled him out, though," said Luke. "I'll ask him that question as soon as he gets back to the city from his assignment."

Tony stared. "You seem to have inside information. Have you been to Leo's office?"

"Misty has," said Luke.

Tony turned and seemed to see Misty in a whole new light.

"Leo was dear to me," she said. "I owe it to him to ensure he gets justice. So, outside work, did Leo have any enemies?"

"No. Everyone liked Leo. Always in good humor, he was a popular guy."

"Did Leo have a will?" asked Luke.

"Yes, he did, but I have no idea what's in it. The reading is this afternoon at Gillespie and Finch downtown."

Once the questions had been exhausted, Misty gave Tony a Tarot reading before he left. The cards raised a lot of questions and didn't provide any answers.

After they saw Tony to the door, Luke took her into his arms. "What do you think, sweetheart? Does Tony know more than he's telling us?"

"His demeanor seemed extremely guarded, and if he was lying, he is very good at it. The cards indicated he might have been holding something back, but I can't say what it might be."

"I didn't feel he was dangerous, though. I can usually feel violence if a person is filled with it."

Misty agreed with that. "No, Tony certainly didn't kill Leo. He loved his older brother."

Louisiana Forest

Ben left Rowanne relaxing in the new shelter he'd made for her. He wasn't sure about abandoning the shack he'd lived in for how long? His memory often played tricks on him. His brain showing him faces of people he didn't know and had never seen before. It was weird, and he hated it when it happened. Lately, it had been happening less and less, and he was thankful for it.

Jogging, it took Ben an hour to cover the distance they had run in the dark in a few minutes. Of course, they'd taken a short cut by jumping off the cliff into the lake.

He had to go back to get their things. They had next to nothing, but he needed his bow if he wanted to feed them.

Before approaching the shack, Ben skirted around in the woods for a half-hour to make sure there was no one in that part of the forest.

Once he listened carefully and heard no sound for ten minutes, he sneaked in the back way and picked up Rowanne's backpack, her boots, his bow and arrows, and the two tins of beans, the can of stew, opener, and spoon.

He pulled on his boots, rolled everything except the backpack inside the thin mattress and blanket, and tied the roll tightly with his belt. He hoisted Rowanne's pack onto his back, picked up the bulging roll, and sneaked out the way he'd come.

Iberville, New Orleans

"I feel like a spy," Misty said as they sat in the truck outside the lawyer's office. "Maybe we should have stayed at home and sent Daddy on his own."

Luke chuckled. "It's not like he's going to get caught. Nobody can see him."

"I know, but I thought we should show him some support. I hope he remembers the important points. Lately, his memory seems cloudy."

"How long do you think he'll stay, sweetheart?"

"Oh, I don't know. Probably a couple of hundred years."

Luke's head turned as he pegged her with a wide stare. "Is that how long ghosts stay when they're haunting? Wow. I'm obviously not up to date on my ghost stats."

Misty giggled.

Louisiana Forest

Rowanne was asleep in her little lean-to when Ben came back with all of their stuff rolled up in the mattress. Nixa jumped up and barked a couple of times, then wagged her tail and ran to Ben. "That was a long walk for you, Ben. Especially carrying all that stuff. You must be tired."

Ben shrugged. "I say, we unroll our mattress and then split a can of beans."

"I could eat." Rowanne helped him untie the mattress and climbed onto the pad. "I'm thinking I should learn how to hunt and help feed us. I don't want to be a burden to you."

"We do need more food to feed two of us, but I was tired of being alone. I'm glad you're here. You're not a burden."

"How long were you alone?" asked Rowanne.

"Always," said Ben. "I've always been alone, remember? I woke up, and here I was, just me."

"That's strange."

Nine Saint Gillian Street

Luke straightened at his desk in his room doing background searches on Gisele Thibodeau, Jamie Wolfe, and Craig Gibson. Stretching side to side, he pulled at the tension in his muscles and took a moment to acknowledge the pain in his back.

Misty stuck her head in the door. "Daddy's back from the lawyer's office."

Luke glanced at the time on his computer screen. "It's been hours, Mist. Where the heck was he?"

"He's not saying. Maybe he took a detour to the dark side and back again. Do you want to hear about the will?"

"I do. I'll come down and finish this later."

"Are you doing the background checks?"

"Uh-huh."

"Why don't you pass them on to Casey. He told me was doing background searches for Blaine at the Agency. He can finish those and give you a break."

Geez, a break sounded good.

"Yeah, I am feeling a bit overwhelmed right now." Luke trudged downstairs and joined Misty in the sitting room. He glanced around as he came through the door and saw no sign of Josiah. He'd only started to be able to see and hear Misty's father a few weeks ago. He hoped he hadn't lost his ability with all the stress. "Is your father here?"

"He's here, but too worn out from the trip to manifest."

"Did he say that?" Luke grinned.

Misty sipped her tea. She hadn't eaten a single thing for breakfast and barely anything since. While they waited to hear what Josiah learned, he went over and popped down a slice of rye bread.

"What did you hear, Daddy?"

"Leo Pinoit was a very wealthy man, Mystere. From what I gathered, he left most of his estate to his younger brother."

"Tony is his only relative."

"What about the townhouse?" Luke put a light layer of strawberry jam on the toast and set it in front of Misty.

"The townhouse goes to Tony."

"I guess that means Craig will be moving out," said Misty.

"Mr. Finch told Tony that up until two weeks ago, Craig was named in the will. Then, without explanation, Leo made an appointment, came into Mr. Finch's office, and cut Craig completely out."

"Did the lawyer give a reason?" asked Luke.

"None. Tony asked the same question, and Mr. Finch said that Leo had his reasons, but he didn't share them."

"Ooh," said Misty, taking a cautious nibble at her toast. "What were the reasons, Leo?"

Leo didn't answer.

"Was Craig at the reading?" asked Misty.

"He was there doing his usual 'drama queen' routine," said Josiah. "When he heard he'd been cut out of the will, he broke down and wept uncontrollably."

"He was playing the bereaved assistant and supportive best friend, overwrought with emotion."

"He used half a box of tissues." Josiah laughed.

Misty was right. The eerie sound that Josiah made when he laughed was unnerving.

Misty took a sip of her tea, and he knew she was only eating to please him. He appreciated it but wasn't trying to punish her. He took a big bite, and she nodded, thankful to not have to eat so much. "Could Craig have killed Leo thinking he would inherit, not knowing Leo had changed his will?"

Luke made a face. "Possibly. Greed is a strong motive."

"Or maybe he *did* know and was angry at being cut out."

"Maybe. I'm not sure Craig could kill anyone, but if he did, I imagine poison would be a weapon of choice."

"Poison is passive-aggressive in a lethal way," said Misty.

"You could say that." Luke winked at her.

Louisiana Forest

After sharing a tin of beans, Rowanne moved a respectful distance away from Ben and lit up a smoke. "This is the last one, Ben. I need to get out of here soon, or I'll go into nicotine withdrawal."

"What's that like?" Ben wore a concerned look.

"It's like… all you can think about is smoking when

you know you can't. You get cranky and aren't the nicest person to be around."

"I think I'll still like to be around you."

Rowanne winked at him. "Tell me everything you can remember from the day you first came to the forest."

"Why?"

"I want to figure out where you came from. What if you have family looking for you all this time?"

"I don't."

"Do you know that for sure?"

"No."

"Start from the first thing you remember in the woods."

Ben sat down cross-legged beside her, and she moved her hand so that he wouldn't get smoke in his face.

"Okay." He touched his filthy, ragged shirt. "That first day, my clothes weren't ripped and dirty, and they fit me better. My boots weren't worn out, and they weren't so tight on my feet like they are now."

"You grew since you got here," said Rowanne. "I'm sixteen, and you look about the same age as me." She checked the bottom of his pant legs. "Your jeans are telling me you grew a couple of inches since you've been here. How much do boys grow in a year?"

"Don't know."

"Me neither, but I could find out if I had my laptop or my phone. Of course, I'd also need the internet."

"Where did you lose them?" asked Ben.

"The bad men in the suits took them away from me when they took me prisoner."

Ben made a pained face. "Before they sold you to the bad man who... hurt you?"

"Yep. Before that, or I could have called for help."

"I'm sorry they hurt you."

She nodded. "I refuse to dwell. They don't deserve any more power over me. I'm alive, and I'm a fighter."

Ben stared into her eyes, making her uncomfortable.

Rowanne squirmed under his steady gaze. "What? Is there dirt on my face?"

"I never kissed a girl before. No girls to kiss."

Rowanne relaxed. Ben was honest, pure, and... disarming. When she spent time with him, she forgot about the bad man and that other stuff. "I'm here now. You can kiss me if you want to."

"Yep. I want to."

"Move closer to me," said Rowanne.

Ben skootched over closer and waited.

Rowanne took his face in her hands and gave him a long, gentle kiss.

When she eased back, Ben's grin spanned ear to ear. "I like kissing you, red-haired girl. Can we kiss more?"

Nine Saint Gillian Street

After lunch, the students returned to the attic and settled around the worktable in their usual spots. Claire tapped the end of her pen on her notepad. "This afternoon, we're going to concentrate only on finding Rowanne. We'll use the athame, and Gran has come up with a couple of drawings Rowanne made as a child. We'll try those because we have nothing else. She took all of her belongings with her."

"We have to find her soon," said Casey. "When people go missing and aren't found within hours, often they never get found."

Michele sneered at him. "You're full of hope and good news, aren't you?"

"I study criminology. It's a fact. What's the point in ignoring the facts and fostering false hope."

"Thank you, Casey," said Claire. "All the more reason for urgency, wouldn't you say, girls?"

"Yes," said Charlotte. "Let's get to work."

"Write down everything you can remember when your vision is over," said Claire. "Perhaps we can put pieces of the puzzle together by the time Luke and Misty come back from the police station."

Detective Scarlett's Office, NOPD

"Thank you for the email, Detective Scarlett," said Luke. "You've identified one of the men in the sex trafficking ring?"

She pushed an eight by ten glossy across her desk. "After weeks of surveillance, we've come up with this guy. His name is Roland Rancourt. He's a successful Louisiana businessman who owns a large company specializing in precast concrete products. We have his home under surveillance and know for certain there are no girls there. Our research department is trying to find any other properties he owns. Then those will be searched systematically as well."

"Is he running this operation solo?" asked Luke.

"We're sure he couldn't be running anything this big alone. It's a network underneath him. Recruiters, handlers, people who screen the clientele. It's big business."

"Has his house been searched?" asked Luke.

"We don't have enough solid evidence to obtain a warrant to search his residence."

"How did you zero in on Mr. Rancourt?" asked Misty.

"We received a tip from an employee at one of the major hotels. A lady on the housekeeping staff observed things she wasn't comfortable with and came forward. Since then—a few weeks ago—they haven't returned to that hotel."

"Most of the operations move the girls constantly," said Luke. "Lower-end operations use truck stops, highway rest areas, and cheap motels. Those aiming for a bigger payday frequent the larger hotels, and some rent secluded estate properties where they have little chance of being discovered. Those are more difficult to track down if they're isolated."

"You have experience in this area, Ranger Hyslop."

"Unfortunately, yes. Not something I like to think about in connection with my niece, but at the Blackmore

Agency, we've dealt with human trafficking."

Nine Saint Gillian Street

After ten minutes of uninterrupted meditation, Claire opened her eyes and began writing on her notepad.

"Did you see where Rowanne is?" asked Diana.

"Possibly, but in an area that huge, she would still be hard to find."

"What kind of an area?" asked Casey.

"Acres and acres of land and trees, lakes and rivers," said Claire. "No houses. Nothing but wilderness."

"Where would that be near New Orleans?" asked Charlotte. "Do we have a map?"

"It has to be out of the city," said Claire.

"I can pull up a state map on my computer," said Casey. "Let me run down to my room and get it."

"Gran saw lots and lots of trees," said Michele. "When she had her first vision."

"True," said Claire, "she did say that."

Casey galloped up the stairs with his laptop and set it up at the end of the table. "Give me a few minutes to look."

"What did you come up with," asked Claire. "Charlotte?"

"I don't know why, but I saw a boy with wild hair, and I think he is helping Rowanne. There were no negative vibes."

"I hope someone out there is helping her," said

Claire.

"So, do I," said Diana. "If I were alone and lost, I'd want someone to help me. I saw lots of trees, and I thought I heard a dog barking."

"That's interesting," said Claire. "How about you, Michele? Anything to add?"

"The only other thing I sensed was a change in Rowanne's attitude. A lot of her anger has faded away. I'm not sure why."

"What have you found, Casey?" asked Claire.

"North of the city, there's a huge tract of state land. It hasn't been developed yet, and there's no public access. Do you think she could be in there?"

"How would she get there?" asked Claire. "If she was running from someone, there would have to be civilization close to it at some point."

"Okay, looking for houses close to it," said Casey. "Here at the southwest end. There is a golf course with a dozen estate homes. The back property line of each of the estates butts up against the edge of the state land."

Claire nodded. "Well done. Let's run it by Luke and see what he thinks."

Louisiana Forest

Rowanne rested for an hour on the mattress, watching over Ben as he slept. She knew his long hike back to his former home had taken a lot out of him even if he wouldn't admit it. And for what, to retrieve their meager possessions? She stroked Nixa's fur and listened to Ben breathe. Rustling through the leaves on the other side of the trees made her jump, and Ben woke up.

Rowanne patted his arm. "Sorry. It's nothing. Just a squirrel or a chipmunk. Go back to sleep."

Ben closed his eyes and went back to sleep while Rowanne concentrated on sending a message. She hadn't been this relaxed since she ran away, and it was a good time to muster her positive energy and send a message to her Uncle Luke.

Nine Saint Gillian Street

Luke parked the Ford Expedition in the back lane and turned off the engine. The silence was precious, and he hated the idea that they had to go inside and face the cyclone of problems whirling around them. Leo, Sam, Rowanne... "Will our lives ever settle down? It seems that since the day I got here, we've had very little time to enjoy one another."

Misty giggled and placed a hand on her belly. They'd stopped at the Walmart pharmacy, and Misty had used the bathroom to pee on the pregnancy test baton. It looked like they were, indeed, expecting.

"I think we've had some time to enjoy one another."

Luke grinned. "I'm so, fucking stoked, Misty, but I'm also terrified. A baby. I still haven't wrapped my head around it."

Misty yawned. "Man, who knew making another person could be so tiring. The day has barely started, and I'm tired and ready to head upstairs for a nap."

Luke drew a deep, steadying breath and exhaled. He wanted this to go well. "It could be your body telling you to slow down. You should listen. Take care of our baby."

Misty smiled. "I'll take care of him."

"Him?" Luke's eyes widened, and he took her hand. "Do you know something I don't?"

"Nope."

"You'd tell me if you knew something, wouldn't you?"

"Sure, I would."

Sure she would. Of course, she would. "Okay, promise me you'll make an appointment for the first of the week. You need a checkup and a baby doctor."

"I promise." Misty opened her door, and Luke sat frozen.

He held up a hand, closed his eyes, and let the vision come to him. It had happened a couple of times before but not often enough to make it commonplace.

Rowanne, with her flaming red hair was lying on a mattress with a boy who was sleeping, and a brown and cream hound dog lay between them.

All around them were trees—nothing but trees. When the images faded, he committed everything to memory.

When he opened his eyes, Misty was right there. "Did you have a vision, sugar? Your face is pale."

"I saw Rowanne. She's with a homeless boy and his dog."

"But she's alive?"

"Yes. And she's pretty happy. Whatever happened, she's gotten free of it for the time being."

Misty smiled. "Then let's find her and bring her home."

They rushed into the kitchen, and Casey, Claire, and the girls were waiting for them. "We were waiting for y'all to come home," said Casey. "We have a possible location and want to run it by y'all."

"That's great," Luke said, hope filling him for the first time in days. "Rowanne just contacted me. She's not alone. She has a homeless boy with her."

"I saw the boy too," said Charlotte. "He's helping her."

On Google Earth, Casey showed Luke the estate properties and the state land behind. They explained their impressions and how they thought things went down.

It made perfect sense. He didn't want to bring it up with the kids, but they'd spoken in Detective Scarlett's office about an estate being a possible venue for the sex trafficking ring. If Rowanne was taken to one of these houses, she would have had an ideal opportunity to run straight into the tract of state land.

"That's where she has to be. She's in there somewhere, and all we have to do is find her."

"Which one of these houses, I wonder?" asked Misty.

"Give me a minute and let me see if any of them belongs to Roland Rancourt." Luke ran upstairs to his desk and booted up his laptop. He went through several databases—county assessment, tax department, land registry—and finally, he had it. The third estate past the golf course belonged to Rancourt Holdings.

With the address scribbled on a piece of paper, Luke ran down the flight of stairs and almost tripped over Hoodoo at the bottom. "I've got it. Road trip. We're going to find Rowanne."

"Umm... Luke, sugar. Slow down a sec. It's dark. You can't find her now. You know she's not in any immediate danger, so maybe you should wait until morning."

Luke exhaled and ran a rough hand through his long, auburn hair. "Damn it. I'm not thinking straight. How about it, Casey? We'll set our alarms and leave at six in the morning."

"I'm in."

The girls looked disappointed that they weren't invited to join the search, but they didn't complain.

"Okay, I'm going to spend time with Gran. Thanks, guys, for all your help."

CHAPTER NINE

Thursday, February 9th.

<u>Nine Saint Gillian Street</u>

Luke and Casey had a quick breakfast of scrambled eggs and cornbread with Misty while Angelique made them a care package for the road.

"Please be careful and keep in touch," said Misty. "I can't bear it when y'all are out of my sight."

Luke smiled. "We'll be fine, and hopefully, by the end of the day we'll be back with Rowanne."

"Did you tell Sam about this new development?"

"No. I called it in to Detective Scarlett but was hoping you'd have time to visit Sam today and tell him where we're looking. It might cheer him up."

Misty nodded. "I'll go this afternoon."

"Thanks, sweetheart."

<u>Gator Run Golf Course. North of New Orleans</u>

Luke followed the GPS north of the city for half an hour until the sign for the golf course appeared on the right-hand side of the road.

"There it is," said Casey. "According to the map, the golf course should be first, and then the estates are farther down the road."

"Private and isolated." Luke made a disgusted face and tried not to focus on his professional instincts of what might have happened to Rowanne before she got away. "Perfect spot to bring their clients to protect their reputations."

They passed the golf course and the clubhouse, then the road narrowed, and they came to the line of estate homes. "That's the third one. No vehicles in the driveway."

The gate was open. Luke drove through the trees and parked in front of the triple garage. The house was a huge brick and stone two-story with arched windows and elegantly carved doors facing a small fish pond.

"Let's ring the bell and see what happens," said Luke.

They got out of the truck, punched the buzzer, waited, pressed it again. No one answered. "The chances are high that there is an alarm system in place. But I need to search the house to see if Rowanne has been here."

"How do we get around the alarm?" asked Casey.

"We don't."

Casey chuckled. "Okay. How much time do we have before a response team arrives?"

"This far out in the country, eight or nine minutes."

Casey shook his head. "I'm studying criminology, and you're turning me into a criminal."

Luke laughed. "Sorry about that. You can always

wait in the truck."

"Hells to the no. I'm in all the way."

Luke nodded. "Well, we know the girls would been stashed in one of the bedrooms upstairs, so if I open the door and we run straight upstairs and look as fast as we can, we might make it out before the cops come."

"What if she *has* been here? Then what do we do?"

"Then we go to the local sheriff's office and get ourselves a dog handler. We'll come back and track her from the back of the house to wherever."

"Okay," said Casey. "Ready when you are."

Luke pulled out his lock pick set and had the front door open inside of a minute. The alarm sounded as they stepped into the foyer, and Casey ran right past. Luke tried a couple of quick four-digit codes, and neither one worked.

"Hurry," Luke hollered as the alarm screamed. "There's no stopping that."

Casey bolted up the stairs and ran willy-nilly through the bedrooms. Damn, there were a lot of them. He found one huge bedroom with a bunch of girl stuff scattered everywhere. The room smelled like perfume. Underwear on the floor. Nail polish and hairbrushes, makeup, and toiletries on the dressers and night tables.

Two queen size beds, messed up but not slept in. On the far side of one of the beds, he found Rowanne's suitcase. He recognized it because he'd seen her carry it into Misty's house. He grabbed it and ran down the stairs hollering to Luke. "I've got her suitcase."

Luke was in one of the downstairs rooms, and he came running out with Rowanne's laptop. "Let's get out of here."

Panting for breath, they ran to the truck.

Casey tossed Rowanne's suitcase into the back seat, and Luke placed her laptop on the seat beside it. Luke revved up the big Ford, backed out of the driveway, and stomped the gas. He retraced their route past the golf course to the main road.

As they turned the corner onto the highway, they passed a security company heading their way with lights flashing on the roof of their car.

Casey ducked down in his seat. "How many minutes was that? I had so much adrenaline pumping that I forgot to count."

Luke laughed. "I did too. I'm so happy we found her stuff. We know she's up here somewhere. She has to be close by—at least within a few miles. All we have to do is find her."

Brooktown Sheriff's Office

Luke showed his creds and spoke to the uniformed deputy on desk duty. Without going into details as to why he inquired about a dog handler in the area, he was told there was none.

When they needed dogs—if ever—they brought them out from Hammond or Baton Rouge.

"Okay, thanks," Luke said to the Deputy. As they

walked back to the truck, he wondered what to do next. "Hey, let's grab a burger, then go back and see if the security company is gone. If they are, we'll try to follow Rowanne's path."

"I can eat a burger anytime, day or night. Fries too."

Louisiana Forest

Under the lean-to, Ben sat cross-legged on the mattress and used his knife to sharpen a half dozen new arrows before he went hunting for food. He carefully notched the ends and inserted feathers from the supply he'd collected.

"Should I come and help you hunt?" asked Rowanne.

"No, then the dog will come and scare the game. I'll go."

"While I wait for you, I'll gather wood for the fire and have it ready."

"I brought the matches," said Ben. "You won't have to do a magick trick."

"It's not a trick," Rowanne snapped. "I used my power."

Ben smiled at her. "Okay. I won't take too long. Will you kiss me when I come back?"

"If you bring home food, sure thing."

Ben smiled. "I won't come home until I have some."

When they returned from the sheriff's office, Luke parked the truck in an unused road allowance where it wasn't readily visible and locked it up. He and Casey skirted around the mansion to the back patio doors and began where Rowanne had probably exited the house.

"I'll use the GPS on my phone," said Luke, "so we can find our way back."

"What if we don't find them today?" asked Casey. "Should we sleep here?"

"We can't give up. It would kill my brother to lose her."

"We won't give up," said Casey. "We can come back to the truck at dusk, sleep in the truck, and try again when it's daylight."

With Casey by his side, Luke jogged across the back lawn of the house, climbed the fence, and walked straight into the woods like Rowanne must have done when she was trying to get away from the traffickers.

"If she walked for three days," said Casey, "she could be miles ahead of us."

"I wonder if there are any roads through the park area—like for maintenance crews—or game wardens—or whatever," asked Luke. He stopped for a second to catch his breath. "I should quit smoking. This would be the ideal time."

"Me too," said Casey. "My lungs are already feeling it."

They trudged along in what Luke believed was a straight line. His phone was in and out, the signal growing weaker by the minute.

Experiencing the vastness of the forest and the time it would take to search though miles of trees, Luke realized how unprepared they were. They should've brought camping gear, more manpower, and a couple of dozen other necessities.

Shit. I'm not thinking like a professional. I know better.

University Hospital, New Orleans

Sam Hyslop lay in the ICU, hooked up to two monitors. The beeping and hissing noises made Misty uneasy as she sat in the guest chair beside his bed.

"Any news?" he asked. "I know Luke will tell me right away if Rowanne is found, but I'm lying here imagining all kinds of terrible things happening to her."

Misty touched his hand. "Lukey obtained promising leads from the police department, and he's gone north of the city to search for Rowanne himself. He's hopeful he might have something to tell us by tonight."

Sam blew out a breath. "Thank God, there's something to work on. Can you tell me what they found out? I thought she was gone without a trace."

I can't tell him about the sex traffickers.

"Umm… Luke believes that whatever trouble Rowanne was in, that she's gotten free of it and is now simply lost in the woods of the state park north of the city. A red-headed girl was seen with a homeless boy, and by the accounts of the kids who saw her, they seemed healthy and intact. Luke's gone looking himself, but it's a lot of area to cover, and she's three days ahead of them. As soon as I hear anything more, I'll come to tell you, or Luke will come if he's home."

Sam sighed and smiled up at here. "Thank you. With so many people looking for her, they have to find her soon. That makes me feel a little better."

Louisiana Forest

After hours and hours of tramping through trees and bushes, Luke wondered if they'd ever find her without help. Even the National Guard would have trouble searching this much land.

The sun began to sink, and Luke felt panic in his throat. They were miles from the truck and had no real direction. Not a single trace of Rowanne all day long.

Dusk was coming down rapidly upon them, and Luke berated himself again for not bringing at least the basics for a night in the forest.

Casey was walking ahead of him as they stumbled into a small clearing. There it was. A hunting shack sitting right in front of them.

Luke's heart began to pound when he saw it. "What's this? A shelter for hunters or poachers?"

He ran to the fire pit and felt the ashes. "Cold. I wonder if she slept here overnight?"

"Let's look inside." Casey tried the door, and it wasn't fitted with a lock. He turned the handle and pushed the flimsy door wide open. "One rickety cot, and that's it."

"Smells like wax," said Luke. "A candle burned in here not too long ago."

Luke walked outside and glanced up at the setting sun. "It's a whole day back to the truck, and we don't have flashlights," said Luke. "We'd be hours ahead in the morning if we slept here. We'd waste too much time going back and starting over."

"Sure," said Casey. "Doesn't bother me. I've slept on a bare floor lots of times."

"I'm sorry, buddy. I should have thought ahead and brought camping gear. Sleeping bags and food would have been good too. My bad."

"Yeah, food would've been good. I'm starving."

"I should let Misty know we're not coming home." Luke tried his phone and couldn't get service. "Damn it. There's no service way out here. She's going to be worried when we don't come home and don't call."

"Not much we can do about it, Luke. Send her good thoughts. She'll know."

Rowanne closed her eyes as she took the first bite of the roasted snake Ben nabbed for them. He didn't tell her how. There were no arrows in it. She'd risked a glance when he brought it back with him, and it looked like its head had been bitten off, but it couldn't have been. He must have caught it with his hands.

There was no way she could watch him skin it and get the meat part ready to roast. Better if she didn't witness the process.

She chewed it warily, then opened her eyes and nodded her head at him. "It's not too bad."

He smiled and bit off a big chunk.

After dinner, Rowanne drew a wide circle with a stick around their camp, then placed the rabbits' feet Ben saved at intervals on the circle. She stood looking up at the moon, her hands raised, and chanted her protection spell.

Goddess of the sun and moon
Keep us safe from now till June
Doers of evil, creatures of night
Run away from our camp in fright
So mote it be.

She repeated it three times, then pulled Ben inside the circle and closed the ward. "Stay inside the circle, and you'll be safe," she whispered.

"Okay. I believe you." He kissed her, and she kissed him back, wrapping her arms around him and holding him tight.

Nine Saint Gillian Street

Luke and Casey didn't come back, and they didn't call. Misty began to worry in earnest when darkness fell. She'd checked her phone countless times, and there were no messages. She poured one last cup of tea and waited a little longer, hoping they'd turn up at the door or call or text or... anything.

They didn't.

Misty trudged upstairs, tired and wanting to go to bed, and at the same time wondering how she could sleep with no word from them. "I don't like this, Lukey," she said to her reflection in the bathroom mirror. "Tell me, y'all are okay."

Nothing.

Misty sat on her bed and spread out her Tarot cards in a Celtic Cross. "Let's see what the cards say."

The first card she turned up was the four of swords in the shadow. "Oh, no—imbalance, fighting a lost cause, the other interpretations were equally unsettling. The second card was the six of pentacles, also in the shadow. They don't have enough resources. I hope I'm wrong. One more card, and I'm giving up. This is depressing. Nine of cups. Oh, that's better. Lukey might get his wish and find her after all, but the other cards are telling me it's going to be a hard task."

I'd better sleep.

Louisiana Forest

Luke woke to a sound he recognized but didn't want to recognize. Men arguing in loud voices, and they were close by.

His heart thumped in his chest as he jumped up off the floor and felt for his gun. In the pitch dark, with his Smittie in his hand, he quietly made his way to the closed door of the shack.

The men were right outside, not two feet away. Casey was asleep on the floor and hadn't heard them. Luke leaned down and touched Casey's arm trying not to startle him.

"What?"

"Shh... men are outside. Listen."

"This is where she ran from when we almost had her. I thought she might have come back here, but the place looks deserted. No fire. The ashes are cold."

Luke held his breath and waited for the men to come in. Surprise was on his side if he and Casey were outnumbered.

The door of the shack opened, and a beam of light crossed the wooden floor. Luke reached out, grabbed hold of the man's arm, and tried to snap a cuff on his wrist.

The man was quick. "Look out," he hollered. He jerked his arm back and ran.

Luke ran outside into the pitch dark and couldn't see shit. He pointed his gun into the black night and hollered. "On your knees. Hands behind your heads. Y'all are under arrest." But they were gone. Footsteps retreated into the woods, and Luke had no way of pursuing them in the dark.

He turned and almost bumped into Casey. "They're still after Rowanne. She can identify them. She's in a lot of danger."

"We better find her as soon as it's daylight," said Casey.

Nine Saint Gillian Street

Misty woke in bed alone, and she was frightened for the first time since Luke had come to live with her. She ran her hand over the sheets on Luke's side of the bed and shivered. A bad dream had woken her out of a deep sleep.

Luke and Casey were in a tiny wooden shack, and

three men came to hurt them.

"Lukey, where are you? I want you to come home."

Misty turned her head to check the time. Four a.m.

I'm awake now. I'll never get back to sleep.

Who were the men? Were they looking for Rowanne? Is that why she's hiding in the forest?

The Tarot was right. The task was arduous. Luke should have taken a sleeping bag and food and water with him. He wasn't thinking clearly, and now he wasn't prepared for how hard it was going to be. Stay safe, Lukey.

Louisiana Forest

Rowanne woke with a start. Her hands trembled, and her body had broken out in a cold sweat.

"The men are still after me," she whispered to Ben.

"The forest is quiet. They aren't near us."

"We need to move in the morning," said Rowanne. "At first light, I have to move on."

Ben pulled her close to him and tucked the threadbare blanket around both of them. "You're shaking. Would it help if I kissed you?"

"You are a kissing machine, Ben." Rowanne cuddled closer to him and covered his mouth with her own.

CHAPTER TEN

Friday, February 10th.

<u>Louisiana Forest</u>

At the crack of dawn, Luke and Casey were out of the shack and on the move. Stiff and sore from sleeping on the bare wooden floor, Luke hoped walking the first few miles would work out the kinks in his back and his neck.

"How do we know which way she went from here?" asked Casey.

"We use our tracking skills," said Luke.

"Do we have any?"

"I have some basics. We watch for broken branches, trampled vegetation, and things like that. Signs that somebody passed through the bush at that particular point."

"Okay, I've got my eyes open for signs. Let's go. I have to keep moving to forget about how hungry I am."

"Think how hungry Rowanne must be," said Luke. "That's what I'm thinking about."

"Shit. It's been days. I wonder what she's eating."

"I wish I knew. Maybe she found some berries or the boy she's with helped her find something."

***

Ben rolled up their camp into one neat, tight roll and strapped it across the back of his shoulders. "I can carry this because you're wearing your backpack."

Rowanne smiled at Ben. There was no end to his consideration. "Good plan. Which way should we go? Where did you see the road?"

"Umm…" Ben turned around twice and pointed. "I think it was that way."

"Okay, here we go. Looking for the road. Come on, Nixa."

Luke and Casey trudged for half an hour following a couple of signs Luke had picked up. He'd found a small boot print in some soft dirt next to a fallen log and figured it might be Rowanne's size. Nobody was certain how big the boy was who'd appeared in the visions. There might be a boy with her, or he might be just that—a vision.

They broke through a particularly dense copse of trees, and Casey stopped dead. He held his arm out to hold Luke back. "Jeeze, Luke, that's a huge drop into a lake. They couldn't have come this way. They must have gone around."

"Maybe not if they were being chased by the men," said Luke. "We now know for sure that men are out there looking for Rowanne. If they were running, they might have jumped into the lake and swum to safety. We'll have to go around. It's going to take a lot longer, but I'm not jumping off a cliff and spending the day in cold, wet clothes."

"Good call. I'm not up for that either. You were right about one thing, Luke. We should have brought more stuff for this adventure."

"Damned right we should. I was in too big a hurry and took off without thinking it through. Big mistake."

Rowanne and Ben jogged for the first while until she became tired and slowed down. "Is it much farther to the road?"

"I can't remember. I only saw it once when I was hunting way over here in this part of the forest."

"Why would you come way over here?" asked Rowanne. "It's so far from the shack where you lived."

"If you can't find food near your den, you go farther."

"How do you have such a good memory for some things, but not for where you came from."

"Don't matter where I came from. I'm with you now, and that's where I'm supposed to be."

Rowanne smiled. "Do you believe that's true?"

"I know it." He touched his chest over his heart.

Rowanne teared up. Crazy as it was, it didn't matter that she'd only known Ben for two days, she felt the same way too.

With Nixa running ahead and sniffing the ground, they tramped through a stand of thick sumac, and when they came out the other side, there was the road.

A dirt road right in front of them.

Rowanne squeezed Ben's hand. "You are the god of the forest. My own personal Green Man."

Ben looked down at himself and frowned. "I'm not green."

Nine Saint Gillian Street

Munching on a cracker to settle her stomach, Misty sat at the worktable in the kitchen with Angelique. They were both worrying about Luke and Casey. "We should put a protection spell on them, *ma cher.*"

"*Oui*," said Angelique. "I'll prepare what we need." Angelique stood in front of the step back cupboard, gazing at the store of supplies.

"I want to use bloodroot, castor beans, lily of the valley, and lovage."

Angelique nodded and assembled the jars of ingredients on the table next to the mortar and pestle. While she prepared the mojo mixture, Misty ran upstairs for the Book of Shadows.

She returned, poured herself a cup of tea, and studied the protections spells trying to decide what would work best. "Daddy, what spell would you use to protect Luke, Casey, and Rowanne out in the middle of a forest?"

"Umm… try page three hundred and ten. I think that one is particularly powerful when the boundaries are unknown."

"Thanks." Misty turned the pages slowly, taking care not to tear the age-old parchment. She found the spell and read it over.

"Yeah. I think that will work."

Angelique finished blending the ingredients in the mortar. "How should we send this, Madam?"

"I think I'll call on the north wind from the attic window."

Angelique nodded. "*Oui,* I agree."

At nine that morning, Charlotte, Diana, and Michele arrived for class, and as they hung up their coats in the front hall closet, they peppered Claire with questions.

"Did Casey come home?" asked Diana. "I had a dream that he spent the night in the woods in the dark."

"I believe your dream was correct, dear," said Claire. "Casey and Luke did not come back, and we haven't heard from them. Misty is anxious, and preparing a protection spell at this moment."

"Oh, may we be part of it?" asked Charlotte.

Misty came out of the kitchen carrying the Book of Shadows. Angelique was right behind her with the mortar in her hand. "Yes, you can. The more power we have, the greater our range. I'll use the attic window to reach the north wind."

"Ooh, so exciting," squealed Diana. She ran up two flights of stairs ahead of all the rest.

"Lovely to have so much energy," said Claire.

Misty giggled. "My energy is dragging along the floor, Mother."

They reached the attic, a little out of breath, and Misty

sat down at the worktable and went over the spell one more time. "I'll cast the spell first, then open the window and call the wind to take my offering."

"Come, girls," said Claire. "We have work to do. Let's cleanse the space and cast a circle."

The girls picked up their besoms and swept the room. Claire cleared the table and laid out the altar cloth and the tools they'd be using.

As soon as Claire pronounced the circle closed, Angelique placed the mortar on the altar cloth in the center of the table.

Misty stood up, raised her arms, and cast the spell.

God of the forest
Hear my plea
Protect my loved ones
Far from me
Birch and Rowan
Ash and Oak
Keep evil from them
Enemies choke
May this spell endure
And not be broke
So mote it be.

Claire opened a door in the circle, and only Misty stepped out, holding the Mortar. She raised the attic window and called to the North Wind.

"Hail to the guardians of the north. Keepers of the earth and all its elements. I call you forth to carry my

protection where it's needed most. Heed my call and accept my gifts."

A gusting wind came out of nowhere. Tree branches blew, windows rattled, and with a great churning sound, leaves, twigs, dirt, and weeds were sucked upwards into the sky. Lightning flashed, and thunder crashed as Misty cast the powdery mixture out the window.

She shouted loud enough to be heard over the thunder.

"I thank the North Wind. You honor me with your presence. I am your humble servant and a child of nature. Thank you for heeding my call."

Misty entered the circle and sat down, exhausted.

"Rest now, dear. As soon as I take down the circle, you must go lie down."

Misty nodded. "I will, Mother. I am tired."

"That was fantastic, Madam LeJeune," said Diana. "I've never seen anything so powerful. You were wonderful."

Misty smiled. "Thanks, girls. I hope it works and keeps our family safe."

Diana's young face took on a serious look. "I hope they are protected. We don't know who or what is out there wishing them harm."

<u>Louisiana Forest</u>

For three hours, Luke and Casey battled the forest, trying to find their way down from the cliff and around the large lake that was blocking their pursuit of Rowanne.

Once they were down in the valley, they sat down at the edge of the water to take a break.

Casey lit up a cigarette as he stared at the calm water rippling in front of him. "I see something."

He jumped up, ran to the edge of the lake, and dropped down on his knees. He waved to Luke. "I think they came out of the water here. Look at this."

"They were barefoot at this point," said Luke. "They had to leave the shack in a big hurry."

"But there was nothing in the shack," said Casey.

"The boy—if there is a real boy—might have gone back for their stuff. I can't imagine that they have a lot."

Casey jumped when thunder cracked overhead in a clear blue sky. "What's that?"

A wind came up and swirled around them, covering them in leaves and twigs. The wind funnel only lasted a few seconds, and it was gone.

"What the heck was that?" Casey picked leaves and twigs out of his hair and brushed the dirt off his jacket.

Luke smiled. "That's Misty protecting us. She's using the north wind to heed her call."

Casey's eyes widened. "She can do that?"

"She's extremely powerful."

***

Rowanne and Ben trudged their way down the dirt road, hoping to find a safe place to hide. So far all they'd seen was more forest with that dirt path down the middle. It made walking a lot easier, and Rowanne was grateful for that, at least. Her feet were sore from the unhealed blisters.

"Can we rest for a minute, Ben?"

"Sure." He pointed into the trees. "Let's get off the road while we rest, in case the bad men see us." He turned to his right, tramped for about a hundred feet, pointed to a fallen tree, and they sat down.

"Wish I had a smoke," said Rowanne.

"Do you have money to buy more?" asked Ben.

"I have a bank card in my wallet, but they took my ID away at the big house."

Thunder cracked overhead, and Rowanne jumped and grabbed Ben's hand. "That scared me."

Wind howled and shook the trees in the forest around them, and Ben glanced around warily. Leaves and twigs rained down on them from above, and then just as suddenly as it began, it was over.

"Thank you, Mystere," said Rowanne, smiling up at the sky. "My Uncle Luke's girlfriend, Mystere LeJeune, is the most powerful witch in N'Orlean."

"Did she send the wind?" asked Ben.

Rowanne nodded. "She put a protection spell on us and used the wind to get it here."

"She must be smart," said Ben.

"I doubted her power, and I was rude to her. I need to apologize and learn everything she can teach me. That would be smart."

Ben grinned at her. "You're the smartest person I know."

Rowanne giggled. "I'm the *only* person you know."

After resting by the lake for a few minutes, Luke and Casey trudged on. Another hour and they came to the primitive lean-to attached to two tall trees. Luke stared at the construction. "Rowanne could never make this. The boy in the visions must've done it. There has to be someone with her."

"Where did he come from?" asked Casey. "Is he lost in the forest too, and they just found each other? Was he part of the kidnapping?"

"I don't know. And we won't know the story until we find them."

"Which way do you think they went?" asked Casey.

"No idea. If you're as hungry as I am, I don't know how much longer we can keep walking and searching without food.

"I'm feeling a bit weak, but the water did help."

He stared at the endless forest ahead of them. "Do you think there's a road on the other side? Like... we could drive around on the highway and come in from the short side if Rowanne is walking all the way through?"

"Good thought," said Luke, "but if we go back for the truck, we'll lose two days, and we'll never catch her."

"We have to find food if we're going to keep going. We can't help anybody if we keel over."

Luke nodded. "Right. Food first, and then put a plan into action. Misty could pick the truck up on the golf course road and drive around, but how would I get a message to her?"

"Can you send your Gran a message?"

"I can try. She always knew what I was thinking when I was growing up in the bayou."

"Then let's try it. Couldn't hurt."

Ben and Rowanne rested for a few minutes in a secluded little clearing a few feet from the dirt road. They were about to get going again when a big black wild turkey gobbled close to them. Ben dropped the bedroll and took off running.

Rowanne stood up and watched him zip through the trees. She'd never seen anyone run like that. He was fast and maneuvered the trees like he was a forest animal himself.

Just before she lost sight of him, she'd swear his body shimmered with a magick glow. She blinked, and he was gone. Instead, she saw a large red fox tearing through the trees. She blinked again, not quite sure if her lack of food was making her delirious, or if she'd actually seen what she thought she had.

Rowanne sat heavy on the log and waited for him to return.

The longer he was gone, the more sense it seemed to make.

Ben belonged in the forest. It was his home. That's

why he had no name and no family he could remember. She had magickal powers, why couldn't he?

A few minutes later, Ben came jogging back to her with the turkey under his arm and a big grin on his face.

Should she say something? What does a girl say when she finds out her cute forest rescuer could turn into a fox? She didn't know the etiquette of shifter culture and didn't want to offend him. He'd been amazing, sweet, protective, and taken good care of her. If she could be a witch, why couldn't the rumors of shifters be real too?

Huh, shifters were real.

They were out there just like witches were out there living day to day among the mundane.

She smiled as he plopped down on the log beside her and dropped the turkey at his feet. "Wow. Great catch on the turkey, Ben. You're super fast."

"Faster when I run on all fours."

Rowanne nodded and let it go. He probably knew she'd seen him shift, and wasn't denying it or trying to hide it. It was part of him like being a witch was part of her. She loved the human side of Ben, and could love the animal part too.

"Want to stop and cook that?" asked Ben. "Or want to save it for when we camp for the night?"

Ben's easy smile and devotion to what she wanted and needed warmed her. That little part of her that had held back because it sensed there was something she didn't know—that hesitated to trust him fully because there was 'something' about him he hadn't told her—fell into place.

"I can wait a bit until we find a good spot to stop."

Ben smiled. "Okay. We'll follow the road a little farther."

Rowanne got to her feet and took his hand. "Ben, what happens if we get back to civilization. Do you want to leave the forest if we get out of the park?"

"I want to be with you."

Rowanne squeezed his hand and smiled. "But what about… you know?"

He blinked. Sometimes Ben looked like any other boy she knew and other times, he seemed young and unsure. "I don't know. I never had to think about it until now."

She didn't like him looking so worried. She tipped her head up and kissed him. "I love you just the way you are, and no matter what you decide."

Ben wrapped strong arms around her and held her close. "Me too. I don't want to be separated from you, red-haired girl. I think it would kill me to be alone again."

Luke and Casey sat out of the wind in the lean-to the kids had left behind while Luke tried sending a message to his grandmother. He concentrated hard on what he wanted done with the truck but didn't feel any positive vibes.

He let out a breath when he was finished. "I don't think that worked. I felt nothing."

"Try Misty. You have a good connection with her."

Luke sighed. "I should've tried before I used my energy."

"You're tired and hungry." Casey shifted position on the bed of leaves, and his hand touched something hard and cold. He dug the can out of the leaves and held it up. "We're saved. Please tell me you've got a can opener."

Luke grinned. "Sure. On my Leatherman."

"Got a spoon on there too?"

"Yep. Half a tin of beans each will get us going."

With spirits raised after their meal of cold beans, Luke tried sending a message to Misty. He visualized where the truck was and what he wanted her to do.

Nine Saint Gillian Street

The entire day had passed without a word from Luke and Misty could hardly bear the thought of spending another night without him. After a long soak in a hot tub, she crawled into bed and hoped the protection spell was working. She lay back on her pillow, closed her eyes, and that's when the vision came. Clear and precise exactly like Luke. Detailed instructions there could be no doubt about.

Misty sat up, switched on the bedside lamp, and wrote everything down. When she set down the notepad, she set the alarm for six and let out a sigh of relief.

Lukey needs help. He wants me to come.

CHAPTER ELEVEN

Saturday, February 11th.

<u>Nine Saint Gillian Street</u>

Energized by the promise of seeing Luke in a few hours, Misty was ready to leave right after her first cup of tea. "Are you almost ready, Mother? We should get going. According to the map, it'll take us quite a while to get to the truck, and then hours to drive around to the other side of the forest.

"Is the driver here?"

"Yes, he's waiting out front."

Claire came down the stairs carrying a small overnight case. "I'm ready. Where's your father?"

"I'm here," said Josiah. "Ready for the road trip."

"Do you have the extra set of keys for the truck. dear?"

Misty nodded. "I scooped them off my dresser."

Angelique hurried into the foyer with a container of muffins and a thermos of tea. "For later."

Misty hugged her. *"Merci, ma cher."*

Louisiana Forest

Tired and weakened by lack of food, Luke and Casey slept overnight in the lean-to. They had wanted to cover more ground, but darkness fell sooner than expected in the heart of the forest, and they turned back and decided to stay where they had shelter until morning.

Temperatures dropped with the setting sun, and they had no sleeping bags or extra jackets. It made more sense to stay where they were than wandering around in the woods in the dark and accomplishing nothing.

Ben woke at dawn like he always did and smiled as he watched Rowanne sleep. He'd never been attached to another person before, and he'd never had anybody to love. He glanced around looking for danger and vowed to himself that if anyone came to take her from him, he would shift and rip their throats out.

Rowanne opened her eyes and looked up at him. "Are you watching me?"

He nodded.

She sat up and cuddled into his arms. "I like having you near me. I'm not sure I want to go home."

"I'll go with you. I never had a home."

"Would you? Could you leave the forest?"

"If you were the reason I left, then I think I could." He stood up. "I'll start a fire and roast more of the turkey."

"It was good last night," said Rowanne. "So good."

Gator Run Road

The cab driver dropped them off at the end of the road, right behind Misty's Ford Expedition. Her truck was parked exactly where Luke said it was in the vision. Misty paid the cabbie, and he turned his taxi around and left.

Claire hopped in the passenger seat when Misty unlocked the truck, and Josiah rode in the back seat. "Do we know where we're going from here, dear?"

"I wrote the instructions down," said Misty. "Lukey was clear on the details."

"He got the first part right," said Claire. "The truck was easy to find."

Misty smiled. "He enjoys details."

"I was a detail person myself," said Josiah.

Claire smiled. "You are a prevaricator, Josiah LeJeune. You flew by the seat of your pants in everything you did."

"I'm more precise in death," he argued.

"You're perfect, Daddy." Misty turned the keys and started them off. "We love you just the way you are."

"I'd tear up if I could."

Misty turned the truck around and laughed. "You're the navigator, Mother. Read the map and guide me to the next road."

Louisiana Forest

The early morning air was crisp and clear as Luke and Casey left the lean-to and followed what they thought was the direction Rowanne and the boy had taken.

It seemed to Luke that the kids knew where they were going, and that had to be thanks to the boy because Rowanne wouldn't know her way through this vast wilderness.

"Thank the goddess for that boy helping her," said Luke. "He probably kept her alive. It seems he knows how to live off the land."

"He had a tin of beans. I wonder where he got those?"

"I bet those belonged to the hunting shack. Hunters often leave tins of food for the next person."

"They do?" Casey threw him a sideways glance.

"Well, they do in the mountain men stories I like to read."

Casey laughed out loud. "For sure, then. It's a thing."

They plodded on for a couple of hours, tramped through a thick clump of sumac, and came out the other side to a dirt road.

"I figured there would be a maintenance road through here," said Luke. "State-owned property nearly always has maintenance—at least part-time."

Casey pointed to the dirt. "Footprints. We can see exactly where they went."

Luke blew out a breath. "I think we're getting close."

Rowanne watched as Ben replaced the burnt part of the spit he'd used the night before, then skewered another chuck of turkey meat, and set it in place over the coals.

They'd set up their camp about a hundred feet off the dirt road where they were invisible to everyone. If the men searching for her came back, they'd never see them in passing.

While Ben cooked, Rowanne used his knife and tried her hand at sharpening the end of a stick to make an arrow. Concentrating hard on her task, she was surprised when a vision interrupted her.

"My Great-Gran is talking to me," she said to Ben.

"I don't hear her."

"She's talking in my head."

Ben's eyes widened. "What's she saying?"

"My Uncle Luke is here in the forest looking for us. Watch for him."

"Will he like me?"

"Yes, he definitely will."

Rowanne ran through the trees and looked up and down the road. She didn't see anybody, but the road twisted and turned, and she couldn't see around corners.

"Did you see him?"

"Not yet."

"How will he find us?" Ben was pacing.

"Don't be nervous of Uncle Luke. He won't hurt you."

"Will he make me stay here and take you away?"

"No, he won't do that either. I'm taking you with me." She stood facing him with her hands on her tiny hips. "But, if you don't like it away from the forest all you have to do is tell me, and I'll bring you back."

"Okay. I want to go to your magick school."

Rowanne smiled. "I'll make sure you can."

"Put a marker at the road," said Ben.

"Good idea. What should I use?"

"Umm… use an arrow."

Rowanne laughed. "Like an arrow pointing the way?"

"I don't know about that."

She picked up one of Ben's arrows with the beautiful feathers on the end, ran out to the road, and dropped it in the dirt at the shoulder. It pointed right to them.

Casey lagged behind Luke. He was getting to the point where he couldn't keep up. Their path was never-ending, twisting and turning through the trees—miles and miles of trees.

Luke seemed to have renewed energy and charged along the road like he had somewhere important to be. He was a few feet ahead when Casey wondered if he could take another step. He stared down at the dirt as he put one foot in front of the other, and that's when he saw it.

"Luke, come back," he hollered.

Luke spun around and came running back. He stared down and blinked. "That's a homemade arrow."

"Think it's telling us to go that way?"

Luke bent down, picked up the arrow, and turned into the trees. "I smell food cooking. Smells like turkey."

"I could use a turkey dinner right about now," said

Casey.

"Me too."

Luke tramped a few more feet, pulled back the bough of a huge tree, and there they were sitting beside a little fire. He ran towards them, his heart filled with an unbelievable relief. "Man, you guys are hard to find."

"Uncle Luke, I'm so glad you found us." Rowanne jumped up and ran to him. She collided against his chest, and he hugged her tight. After a long moment, he let her ease back, and he turned to the boy beside her. "This is Ben. He saved my life more than once."

Luke held out a hand to Ben, a wild-looking forest boy with tangled hair and a dirty face. He smelled of smoke and leaves mixed with the hint of an animal scent. "Thank you for taking care of Rowanne."

"It's my destiny to take care of her. She's my mate."

Luke blinked. Okay, that was unexpected. Didn't matter. Now was not the time for a debate. He was nothing but grateful to this kid.

"Casey, are you hungry?" asked Rowanne. "Ben caught a wild turkey for us. It's good. Better than the snake."

Luke smiled at his niece. The Rowanne he knew a week ago would never have taken a bite out of a snake.

"I'm half starved, Row. Have you got extra?"

Ben nodded. "We give extras to Nixa, but you can have some. I don't think she'll mind."

Casey plopped on the ground next to the dog and

accepted the chunk of roasted meat Ben handed him. "Thanks. I mean that. How did you catch this turkey?"

"I ran fast."

"I bet."

Rowanne squeezed his arm, her smile warmer than he'd seen in... he couldn't remember how long. "Uncle Luke, are you hungry?"

Luke nodded. "I've never been this hungry, but it's a good lesson. It makes you thankful for what you have."

Rowanne passed him a chunk of the roasted meat. Grease dripped off her hand, and she giggled. "We have no napkins."

"No problem." Luke ate the big chunk of turkey, and when he finished, he wiped his hands on his filthy jeans. "That was about the best turkey I've ever eaten, son. Well done, Ben."

Ben straightened and smiled.

The compliment earned him another loving smile from his niece. He pulled out his cell and tried again for service. "Still no service. My battery is almost dead."

Casey nodded. "Mine *is* dead. I hope Blaine isn't trying to text me. He texts every day."

"They took my cell and my laptop," said Rowanne, a hint of sadness in her voice.

Luke smiled at his niece. "Good news there, Row. I found your laptop at the estate, and Casey found your suitcase."

"Did you go to that house? How did you find it?"

"I had help from the police department. They have their eye on that bunch already. When I get back, I'm going to help take them down."

"Where are my clothes?" asked Rowanne. "I want to change out of these filthy rags."

Luke understood that. He was three days in and felt gross. She was days longer in the same clothes. "Your case is in Misty's truck. We have to find it first."

Casey pointed out toward the road. "Ben, how far is it to the end of the road?"

"Don't know. Didn't go there. I live here."

"Didn't you want to get out of the forest?"

"Why? I live here."

Rowanne reached over and held Ben's hand.

"How long have you lived in the forest, Ben?" asked Luke.

"Can't remember."

Rowanne rolled her eyes at Luke, and he didn't ask any more questions. "Let's put the fire out and gather up our stuff. We still have a long walk ahead of us." She packed all of her belongings into her backpack and struggled into the straps.

Ben rolled all of their gear into the flimsy mattress, tied it up and strapped it on his back. He picked up his bow in one hand and reached for Rowanne's hand with the other. "Ready."

"Come, Nixa." The little hound ran along beside Rowanne.

The five of them trudged down the dirt road for a couple of hours, hoping to come to the end of the forest. The trees were thick and seemed to go on forever.

While they walked, none of them had much to say. Luke and Casey were exhausted and too tired to talk. Ben was silent and stuck close to Rowanne. Rowanne limped along until she couldn't take another step, her boots rubbing on her blisters. She kicked them off, tied the laces together, slung them over her shoulder, and walked barefoot on the dirt road.

I see a fence," hollered Casey. "I think we're there."

He broke into a trot following the curve in the road, and around the next bend was the gate. Casey stood at the gate wearing a huge smile. When the others caught up, he pointed. "Look who's waiting for us on the other side of the fence."

Luke's face lit up when he saw Misty's truck. He gave her a big wave and hurried over the fence.

As soon as Misty saw them, she was out of the truck and running towards them.

Ben hopped the fence, then helped Rowanne get over. When he saw the truck, he took her hand and pulled her close to him. "I'm scared."

"It's okay, sweetie. I'll sit close to you." Rowanne slipped an arm around his waist and turned to Misty. "This is Ben. He saved my life."

Misty smiled and hugged Ben. "You are a special boy, Ben. I'm so happy to meet you."

Luke opened all the truck doors to let everybody pile

in for the trip back to New Orleans. "Nixa will have to sit in the back."

"You can drive, sugar," said Misty. "I want to sit with Ben and calm him. He's anxious about riding in the truck and leaving the forest."

Ben's big brown eyes fixated on Misty as she climbed into the seat next to him.

"I'll sit in the way-back, Mist, with the dog," said Casey. "All I want to do is close my eyes and sleep."

"Y'all hungry?" asked Misty.

"Not too bad," said Luke. "Ben caught a turkey and roasted it over the fire. Best I've ever eaten."

Ben smiled and turned to Misty. "Rowanne belongs to me."

Misty nodded. "I understand, Ben. Foxes mate for life."

Rowanne's eyes widened, amazed by Misty's power of perception. She never should have doubted her.

"I'm happy y'all are found safe and sound," said Claire from the passenger seat. Your great grandmother has been in quite a state since you left the house."

Rowanne drew a deep breath. "I made a terrible mistake, and I'm sorry for so many things. I'm a lot smarter now. And though some of it was horrible, if I hadn't run away, I never would've found Ben." She squeezed his hand and smiled.

"I want to go to the magick school," said Ben, blinking up at Misty. "I never went to school."

Misty patted Ben's leg. "Of course, you can go to our

school, sugar. Mother would love another student. Especially one as gifted and as special as you are."

Nine Saint Gillian Street

Luke parked the truck in the laneway behind the house and gave a huge sigh of relief that they were all home, safe, and fairly sound. He'd almost lost his mind with worry, but once Sam saw Rowanne in the flesh, they would both be able to relax a little.

"Let's go inside and celebrate. The first thing we need to do is phone Sam and tell him the good news."

Rowanne frowned. "I didn't mean to worry Daddy. I can't believe I was so selfish. I'm sorry, Uncle Luke. I'll go see him in the hospital as soon as I can. I promise I'll make it up to all of you."

Hoodoo bounded towards them as they came through the back door. He stopped short at the sight of Nixa, growled once, then licked the little hound's face.

"That's Hoo," said Rowanne. "He's your new friend."

Luke walked hand-in-hand with Misty and wasn't sure who was holding whom up. "As soon as we shower and change clothes, we'll go to the hospital."

Gran greeted them in the kitchen with tears in her eyes. Rowanne hugged her. "I'm so sorry I made you worry, Gran. I love you so much."

"And is this the young man who saved your life?"

"This is Ben, Gran. He's a very special person."

"I can see how much he means to you, dear. How

lovely."

Misty headed to the bottom of the stairs. "Rowanne, come with me, and we'll show Ben his room. Casey, can you find some clothes to loan Ben to go to the hospital? I'll shop for him later today."

Casey nodded, toed off his filthy boots, and followed Misty upstairs. "Boy, do I need a shower to wash off this grime."

Ben blinked. "I never had a shower. I swim in the lake."

Casey chuckled. "I drank from that lake, Ben. That water is coooold."

"Yes. Water is cold," said Ben.

Upstairs, Misty walked down the wide hallway and opened the door of the one unoccupied guest room. "You can have this room, Ben."

"Is this where Rowanne sleeps?"

"No. Rowanne sleeps across the hall."

"I'll stay with her," said Ben.

Rowanne smiled.

Misty wasn't sure what to say about that. "We better run that by Luke and Gran."

"It's okay, Misty. We'll work it out." Rowanne took Ben's hand and showed him her room.

University Hospital, New Orleans

Sam Hyslop was propped up in bed, waiting for them. Luke had called and told him the news, and he was anxious to see his daughter and the boy who had saved her life in the forest.

Tears filled his eyes when Rowanne walked through the door holding the hand of a handsome teenage boy. Rowanne had never had a steady boyfriend, but the time had come, and Sam had to accept the fact that Rowanne and Ben and been together in the forest for several days and nights. If something had happened between them, it was too late to worry about it now. He didn't want to fight and push her away again.

For now, he'd roll with it.

He held out his arms for his daughter, and Rowanne ran to him and hugged him. She reached out her hand and pulled Ben closer. "This is my Daddy. Daddy, this is Ben."

Sam offered his hand to Ben. "I'm happy to meet you, Ben, and so grateful you took care of Rowanne when she was lost and alone."

"She was sent to me. It's my honor to take care of her."

Sam didn't know what to make of that, but owed the boy everything for saving Rowanne's life.

CHAPTER TWELVE

Sunday, February 12th.

<u>Nine Saint Gillian Street</u>

Misty smiled at Ben and Rowanne when they came into the dining room for breakfast. The fox shifter sat down next to Rowanne, wary, on guard, and ready to cut and run.

After Rowanne spent an hour washing and untangling his hair the night before, Ben looked like a different kid. Civilized on the outside, but Misty worried about the Ben on the inside.

Misty made Ben a plate and set it down for him. "I put bacon and sausages on there, for you, because I expect you're a meat-eater. You're welcome to try anything else you think you might like."

Ben nodded and smiled at her.

"We only ate meat in the forest," said Rowanne. "The meat that Ben caught or shot with his bow and arrows."

Claire smiled at the boy. "I heard a rumor that Ben cooks a mean turkey. What do want to drink, son?"

"I drink water from the river."

Rowanne set her glass of orange juice down and

jumped up. "I'll get water."

"Thank you, dear."

"Your house is big," he said to Misty.

"Daddy bought it for us. He died here, but his ghost still lives here."

Ben nodded. "I talked to him when I woke up. He watched over Rowanne last night."

Misty smiled. "Not everyone can hear or see Daddy."

"He thinks the bad men might come here," said Ben. "We have to watch out for them."

Misty glanced around, checking the four corners of the room to see if her father was there. "Daddy? What were you saying to Ben?"

"Rowanne can identify powerful people in high places," said Josiah. "I fear they haven't given up."

"You're right, Monsieur LeJeune," said Luke. "We can't let our guard down. Not for a minute."

Ben nodded his head and ate six more sausages.

Crescent Park

After another visit to the hospital, Luke and Misty took Ben and Rowanne to Crescent Park. They strolled along the banks of the Mississippi and Ben seemed to relax out in the open.

"He needs to be outside," whispered Misty. "I'm going to put him on tasks in the yard."

"Good idea," said Luke. "I think it would break Rowanne's heart if he went back to the forest."

Nine Saint Gillian Street

Misty made sure there was both steak and chicken for dinner, along with the cornbread and vegetables they usually ate. So far, Ben had only eaten the meat that was offered, and she wanted him to have enough food until he tried a few new things. Up until he'd left the forest, he'd hunted and lived like a fox.

"May I see the magick school?" asked Ben when dinner was over.

Claire nodded. "Rowanne can show you. It's on the top floor, and class will start at nine in the morning."

"Come on, Ben. I'll show you, and I'll get you a notebook."

The pair ran up the stairs and were out of breath when they reached the top. Rowanne led the way into the classroom and showed him the work table and the shelves and cupboards filled with supplies.

"What do I have to do?" he asked.

"Nothing. You listen to what Madam LeJeune tells you, and then you try it. It's not hard, but it takes a lot of practice."

"When I tried to shoot an arrow at first, I didn't hit the squirrels. I did it over and over…like a thousand times."

Rowanne nodded. "Exactly. That's what I'm talking about. You have to pick up your wand and say the spell over and over until you get it to work."

"I don't have a wand."

"Yes, you do. A wand can be any kind of a stick that's

special for you. You can use one of your arrows. Pick the one you like the best to be your wand."

Ben grinned. "I know which one."

"Me too." Rowanne kissed him.

CHAPTER THIRTEEN

Monday, February 13th.

Luke's first appointment of the morning was with Detectives Scarlett and Kroll in their office. He wanted to make a formal statement detailing everything he and Casey had discovered about the sex traffickers, and while he was at the police station, he also intended to let Lieutenant White in Missing Persons know that his niece had been found and brought home.

"Good morning, ladies," he said, leaning into their cubicles. "I have good news for y'all. My niece, Rowanne, is home, and able to positively identify photos of the men who took her."

Kroll straightened at her desk. "Did you bring her with you to make a statement?"

"No, not yet. She spent five days lost in the woods and needs some time to rest and recover. I'd prefer it if y'all could speak to her at home. She's staying with Madam LeJeune and me while her father is in University Hospital."

"I'd like to talk to her as soon as possible," said

Scarlett, "while everything is fresh in her mind."

"Let's try for this evening," said Luke. "If Rowanne's agreeable, I'll give you a call with a time and you can bring the photos of your suspects."

"We have several prominent men under surveillance," said Detective Kroll. "And thank you for the information on that estate they are using north of the city."

Luke shrugged. "It's registered in the name of one of Rancourt's companies. I'm surprised you didn't have it under surveillance already."

Kroll stiffened. "There are a lot of men involved, and they each own multiple properties. It comes down to limited city manpower. We have other open cases, and we're moving as fast as we can."

Luke sighed. "Yeah, I realize how frustrating it can be from working in N'Orlean's homicide."

Detective Scarlett leaned back in her chair. "We sent a forensic team to the estate when we got your call. I'll let you know what they found once the report comes back."

"Thank you," said Luke.

"No, we should be thanking you, Ranger Hyslop. We now have a witness who can positively identify these men when we go to trial. You've helped us make a giant leap forward. And congratulations on finding her and bringing her home."

Nine Saint Gillian Street

Charlotte, Diana, and Michele arrived at eight forty-five

for class and were thrilled to discover Rowanne had been found alive and brought home. Diana seemed especially happy to hear Casey was back too.

Diane bent down and rubbed the little hound dog's head. "A new dog? Aren't you a cute girl."

Claire nodded. "Rowanne found her lost in the forest like she was. She came from the west, and she named her Nixa."

Upstairs in the classroom in the attic, the girls were introduced to Ben.

Charlotte nodded from her seat. "Hi Ben, happy to meet you. Thank you for taking care of Rowanne in the forest."

"It's my destiny to take care of her."

Charlotte smiled at him.

"Do you want to be a witch, Ben?" asked Diana.

"I don't know what a witch does. I want to go to school because I never went to school."

"Never?"

"Nope."

Before Ben became inundated with questions, Claire put on her teacher hat, and took over. "Okay, students, let's start this morning with some practical magick. We'll begin with the basics and practice with our wands."

"For a wand, Ben is going to use one of the arrows he made by hand," said Rowanne.

Claire pointed to it, lying on the table in front of Ben. "It is lovely, Ben. Fine workmanship, child."

"Thank you."

"What beautiful feathers, Ben," said Michele. "What birds are they from?"

"The blue one is from a heron, and an ibis gave me one of the white ones. The owl who lives in the tree above my house gave me the striped one."

"Ben has friends in the forest," said Rowanne.

He smiled and picked up his arrow.

Claire picked up her wand and held it out in front of her. "Ben, the way we use our wand is like this. We use the wand as an extension of our own arms. What I want you to try, is to focus all of your energy—and I sense you have a lot of it—down your arm, into your hand, through your fingers and out through the tip of your beautiful arrow."

Ben nodded. He stood up, squinted his eyes as he concentrated hard, and pointed the arrow at the opposite wall. A fireball the size of a baseball flew across the room and blasted a fiery hole in the wall.

"My goodness," said Claire with a big smile on her face. "We'll have a job harnessing all that power." She hurried over to the wall and put out the fire with a few swats from her besom.

Ben grinned. "Can I be a witch like Rowanne?"

"You certainly can, dear. Misty will have to teach you how to control your power and use it wisely."

Rowanne gave Ben a thumbs up. "Fantastic, Ben. You will be lighting candles in no time."

"I want to light a candle like Rowanne did at my

house. Can I light a candle?"

Claire nodded her head. "Michele, dear, fetch some candles from the supply cupboard, and we'll all practice a fire spell."

"Ooh," squealed Diana, "this will be so much fun."

Rowanne hopped up and helped Michele set the candles in front of each student.

"Do y'all have a favorite fire spell you can use?" asked Claire. "If not, I can find one for you in the Book."

"I'll start with the one Misty gave me," said Casey. He held out his elegant wand embedded with crystals.

> *Candle wax with smoke and fire*
> *Ignite, I beg you*
> *Flame burn higher*
> *So mote it be.*

With a small poof, Casey's candle ignited, and he beamed a proud smile.

Ben nodded his approval.

They each took turns around the table until it was Ben's turn.

"Go ahead when you're ready, Ben," said Claire. "A spell is just words. You can use any words that work for you and accomplish your goal."

> *Fire come down from the sky*
> *Light my candle*
> *Flame burn high*

Ben pointed his wand, and the candle burst into flame.

Everyone clapped for Ben, and he beamed.

"Fantastic, Ben," said Rowanne. "I knew you could do it."

"Am I a witch?"

"One step closer," said Claire. "Keep practicing, and you'll be there before you know it."

"Thanks," said Ben. "I want to be a witch like Rowanne."

Misty and Angelique worked on packing orders in the kitchen. The online business for Misty's healing products had taken off, and they could barely keep up with the demand.

Orders for Angelique's love potion poured in every day, and she worked diligently brewing up batch after batch to maintain her supply.

"I'm putting the kettle on," said Misty. "We need a break."

Her cell signaled a text as she crossed the kitchen, and she hoped it was from Luke. It wasn't.

"You lied to Leo. You crazy witch. I'll make you pay."

"Ooh," said Misty, "somebody is mad at me."

"Who?" asked Angelique.

"I don't recognize the number. I'll get Lukey to find out who it is."

***

Luke was halfway home from the police station when Misty called. "What, sweetheart? Are you feeling all right?"

"Yes, but I got a strange message, and I wonder if you could find out who doesn't like me."

"Was it a threat?"

"I'll read it to you." Misty read Luke the message.

"What number did it come from?" asked Luke. He pulled over to the curb so he could write it down. "Okay, I've got it. I'll see where it came from."

"Thanks. I love you."

Luke ran the number through one of the data bases available to him and got his answer. Gisele Thibodeau, Leo's old boss. He turned at the next corner and drove downtown to the magazine Leo used to work for.

Incensed by the threat and fiercely protective of Misty, Luke barged past Gisele Thibodeau's assistant and headed straight for the magazine editor's door.

"You can't go in there, sir. Ms. Thibodeau is busy."

Ignoring the warning, Luke opened the door and barged in. He recognized the man in the guest chair. Gisele was engaged in a conversation with Jamie Wolfe. They both turned to see who had burst into the office.

"Who are you?" asked Gisele. "I don't know what makes you think you can—"

Luke pointed a finger, and she shut up. "Ms. Thibodeau, you have an appointment with the police. You cannot threaten someone and get away with it."

She reached for her cell, and Luke snatched it from her hand. "This is all the evidence I need. Hold your hands out in front of you."

Gisele screamed and tried to run, but Luke had hold of her wrist. He snapped a cuff on and didn't let go.

"Call the police, Jamie," screamed Gisele.

Luke glared at her. "I *am* the police. I'm taking you to headquarters."

"I'd like to see some identification," said Jamie Wolfe. He didn't seemed worried that his boss was in handcuffs. Luke finished reciting the Miranda and showed Wolfe his creds. Jamie chuckled. "Texas Ranger in New Orleans. Sounds like a TV series."

"I want my attorney," shouted Gisele. "I have rights."

Luke smiled. "I just told you what they were. You will be afforded the opportunity to call your lawyer, ma'am. As soon as I book you for threatening Mystere LeJeune."

Nine Saint Gillian Street

Rowanne and Ben were seated in the front parlor with Misty when Detectives Scarlett and Kroll, from the sex crimes unit came at seven.

Luke greeted them at the door and took their coats. "Y'all can speak to my niece in here."

"Thank you," said Kroll. She smiled at Rowanne and Ben as she walked into the room. "I'm happy to meet you, Rowanne. You've been through quite an ordeal."

"Yes, ma'am," said Rowanne. "If it wasn't for Ben, I

would have died in the forest."

"Then, this young man is a true hero."

Ben appeared frightened of the two women. Misty felt the panic radiating from him, stood up, took Ben's hand, and led him out of the room.

Detective Scarlett turned to watch Ben leave and said, "We'll need his statement too."

"No," said Luke, "you won't. He only met my niece when she ran into the forest. He has nothing to do with what happened before her escape."

"You didn't know him before you ran into the forest?" asked Kroll.

"No," said Rowanne.

"Let's start from when you left this house and ran away. Could you do that?" She turned on the recorder, and Rowanne began her story.

When she finished, Detective Scarlett had a few questions. "The three girls you were with, Evey, Bridgette, and Mia, did they give a last name or say where they were from?"

Rowanne shook her head. "No, but I could tell they'd been prisoners for a long time."

"Uh-huh."

"We brought some pictures for you to look at," said Scarlett. She unzipped her briefcase and pulled out several eight by tens. She spread them out on the table in front of Rowanne. "Take your time and tell me if you see any of the men who kidnapped you."

Rowanne studied the pictures and then pointed to two

of them. "Him. I think he was the boss. He gave the girls orders. They called him Malcolm, but I don't know if that's his real name or not." She pointed to a picture of another man in a designer suit. "This guy was at the party at the estate, but he wasn't at the hotel."

"Fantastic," said Detective Kroll. "You did well, Rowanne. I hope we can find the men and return the rest of the girls to their families."

"I tried to make the girls run when we had the chance," said Rowanne, "but they were too afraid of what the men would do to them if we got caught."

"It happens. After they try to escape a few times and are punished, they give up trying. Hopefully we'll arrest the men soon, and the girls won't have to be afraid any longer."

"What about the boys in the gangs who are grabbing the girls off the street and selling them to these men," asked Rowanne. "Are you trying to find them?"

"Yes, we are."

"Okay, good," said Rowanne. "They were liars, and they were mean."

"Gang members," said Detective Scarlett, "but we'll catch them all eventually."

Luke showed the detectives out and locked the door behind them. "I bet you're glad that's over."

"Wasn't too bad," said Rowanne. "I'm not sure if they were good cops. You could probably catch the men faster than they could, Uncle Luke."

"I'm working on it. I have some feelers out there."

"I'm betting on you," said Rowanne. "I better check on Ben. I think the policewomen scared him."

"Misty knew he was afraid and rescued him."

"She's incredible, with him. She knew who he was the minute she met him. I was wrong about her, Uncle Luke. I'm happy for you. I can see how much you love her."

"Thanks, honey. We are happy together."

Rowanne ran down the hall to the kitchen and found Ben making poppets with Angelique. She stood in amazement, watching him. "I didn't know you could sew."

"He's good with his hands," said Misty. "A natural crafter."

"I made a red one for you," said Ben. "Angelique is sewing the eyes on."

Rowanne giggled "That is so cute. Thank you."

"I'm a witch," said Ben. "I can do magick like you."

Rowanne hugged him from behind and kissed his neck. "You *are* magick, Ben. You transformed me."

CHAPTER FOURTEEN

Tuesday, February 14th.

Valentine's Day.

<u>Nine Saint Gillian Street</u>

Misty cried out before dawn. She thrashed around in the bed and woke herself up from a bad dream.

Luke held her in his arms and tried to calm her. "It was only a dream, sweetheart." He stroked her long hair. "Only a dream. You're awake now."

"She's so angry," said Misty.

"Who?"

"Gisele Thibodeau."

"I charged her with threatening you, but I'm afraid what she said in the text wasn't enough to keep her locked up."

"In my dream, Gisele told Leo she was in love with him. Leo laughed at her when she told him how she felt and made matters worse by telling her he was seeing someone else. The woman was there standing beside Leo, but I couldn't see her face. I don't know who it was."

"The police will eventually find the killer, Mist. You don't have to do it. We have enough going on right here at home."

Luke's words didn't pacify her. "Gisele is furious with me, Lukey. Maybe she had to kill Leo because he didn't want her, and she's blaming me."

"Nobody *has* to kill anybody. If she killed Leo, it was because she couldn't have him and didn't want anyone else to have him. Unrequited love is a motive as old as time itself."

"But do the police have any evidence she poisoned him? Jamie brought the wine, and the poison was in the wine."

"Gisele could have put the poison in after the bottle was opened. Maybe she stopped by to have Leo sign something or joined him for a drink."

"I guess so," said Misty, not sounding convinced. "If someone put the poison in Leo's glass after the wine was opened, it could have been any guest in his home."

"It's tough, Misty, but you have to accept the fact that maybe we don't have enough information to find Leo's killer. Unless something new comes to light, we might have to wait to find his justice for him."

Misty let her head flop back onto her pillow. "I'll never give up. Leo was a good man, and I'll figure it out."

Luke kissed her cheek. "I have no doubt about that. We'll get the killer, sweetheart. I promise."

"Thanks, Lukey. You're my rock."

Luke kissed her again, nuzzling the soft line of her jaw toward her ear. "Do you know what day this is?"

"Nope. I've lost track."

"In the mundane world, it's Valentine's Day."

"Ooh, I completely forgot." Her hands slid down his bare ribs as she pulled him closer. "Come here Valentine, and show me how much you love me."

Luke laughed as she went for his boxers. "But, I have a card with a sparkly heart on it to show you how much I love you."

Misty laughed. "Not good enough."

He lifted his hips so she could gain access to what she wanted and laughed. "All right, then. We'll do this your way."

Misty giggled. "Such a smart man."

The girls arrived for class just before nine, and Claire greeted them in the foyer and chatted with them as they hung up their coats. "Because it's Valentine's Day, we're going to be kitchen witches today. Angelique has everything ready for us, and we'll be making her famous love potion."

"Yay!" Diana squealed. "I was hoping we'd do something extra special for Valentine's Day. I love coming to school because every day is different and exciting."

Claire smiled. "I'm glad y'all feel that way. It makes it so much easier for me."

Rowanne and Ben were already seated at the worktable with the recipe in front of them.

"We'll work in twos," said Claire, "because the stove will only hold three cauldrons at a time. "Diana can work with Casey, Charlotte, and Michele together, and Ben and Rowanne.

All the ingredients you need are in this cupboard," Claire pointed to the antique step back lined with jars and bottles. "Read the labels carefully, and when the batches are blended and cooled, we'll bottle it all and pack the waiting orders. It will be a learning project, but we'll also help Misty and Angelique get caught up with the online orders."

"I looked at our web page online," said Casey, "and 'Misty's Magickal Mojo' is pretty impressive. Who designed the page?"

For a moment, Misty looked like she might tear up. "Blaine designed it when I lived in Austin."

Casey nodded. "He's stellar on the computer."

"Do you miss him a lot?" asked Misty.

"When this course is over, I have to go home and help him. He has too much work."

"I'll be sad when you go home," said Misty.

"I'll be sad too. I love it here in New Orleans, but I miss Blaine and Carm and Farrell. I have two families now where only a little while ago I didn't have any."

Upstairs at his desk, Luke accessed the latest reports on the murder of Leo Pinoit. He read through the files twice and wasn't happy. The lead Detective on the case, Andy Rislow, liked Craig Gibson for the murder, but he couldn't come up with any evidence. He had interviewed Gisele Thibodeau but passed her over as a suspect.

"I wonder if the detective knows about Leo changing his will and cutting Craig out?" Something happened between the two of them two weeks before the murder, but no one knew what it was. And what about Jamie Wolfe?

There was more to this, and he knew a dead end when he saw one. Should he call and interfere? Would Detective Rislow even believe the facts they'd gathered?

Not everyone accepted the psychic and mystical side of what Misty and he could do. He didn't know enough about the Detective to venture a guess.

He'd leave it for now. He promised Misty they'd keep at it, and they would. Leo would find his justice. It just might not be as swift as they'd hoped.

Everything in due time.

<u>University Hospital</u>

Luke arrived at the start of visiting hours and found that his brother had been moved into a different room on the cardiac floor. Sam grinned when Luke walked through the door. "I'm moving up in the world. One less machine attached to me."

"I'm happy you're doing better," said Luke. "Any word on when you're getting out of here?"

"Possibly Sunday if I behave myself," said Sam. "How's Rowanne?"

"Great. She gave her statement to the detectives, and she did well. Calm and cool. A lot of her negative attitude got lost in the forest, and I think it has everything to do with Ben."

Sam frowned. "What kind of situation is that? I have to worry. Do you think they are... having sex?"

"I don't think so, but truthfully, I have no idea. Teens nowadays have sex sooner than they used to in our generation. Ben and Rowanne were in the forest for days and nights all alone. Who knows what happened?"

"They seem close," said Sam. "A little too close for my liking."

"After the trauma she suffered, Rowanne needed someone to bond with, and Ben was there."

"He's her first boyfriend," said Sam. "I guess I could call him that although he seems a little..."

"A little what?" asked Luke.

"Oh, I don't know the right word for it. Non-worldly."

"He's a forest dweller, Sam. Ben is a shifter."

Sam's mouth widened into a grin. "You always filled me full of bullshit when we were kids, Lukey. I stopped falling for it years ago."

Luke shrugged. "I didn't question Rowanne on the subject, but Misty knew it as soon as she touched him."

Sam shook his head, and Luke knew he didn't believe him. Didn't matter. They didn't agree on a lot of things. It didn't change the truth of it.

"Misty is something else again, Luke," Sam said, his voice cautious. "She's beautiful and nice enough, but she gives off some extremely freaky vibes."

"She's a very powerful witch. That's magick you're feeling."

He shrugged. "Look, you can believe what you want, but are you sure you want to get so close to her?"

Luke stiffened and drew a steadying breath. "Too late now, Sam. I'm hopelessly in love with her. We're having a baby."

He gave Sam a moment to digest that and hoped his brother could be supportive. He didn't want another line drawn in the sand between them. He wanted to be closer to him, especially after all this near-death drama.

After a moment, Sam held out his hand. "Well, all right then, that's settled. That is wonderful news, Luke. I couldn't be happier for you—for the both of you."

"I'm beyond excited."

"When is the baby due?"

"Hallowe'en."

"Of course," said Sam. "I should have guessed."

Nine Saint Gillian Street

The aroma of jambalaya bubbling on the stove greeted Luke when he came home from the hospital. The dining room table was set for a feast, and all the ladies were busy in the kitchen.

Luke joined Casey and Ben in the back garden, where they were pulling dead weeds and cleaning up all the winter debris. "Hey guys. You pull yard duty?"

Casey grinned. "We're going to get paid off with a

big Valentine's dinner. Can't wait for Misty and Angelique's Cajun cooking."

"I was raised on Cajun," said Luke. "My Gran was a whiz in the kitchen when she was younger, and she baked fresh bread a lot. It was her specialty. Love the smell of it in the oven." Luke took a big breath, thinking of the smell of the bread.

Ben wasn't listening to their conversation. The boy took a step closer to the pond and stared down at the fish swimming in circles.

Luke lit up a smoke and watched, wondering if he might reach in and nab himself a fish.

Valentine's dinner was a huge success. Fun and laughter and delicious food. Claire baked a red velvet cake for dessert and decorated it with pink icing and red cinnamon hearts. After dinner, Misty served coffee in the front parlor, and she and Claire gave everyone Tarot readings.

Luke sat back and let go of the tension he'd been feeling since Rowanne ran away. It was good to relax and spend time with the people he loved.

Maybe he and his brother would be closer when Sam was released from the hospital. That would make things perfect.

CHAPTER FIFTEEN

Wednesday, February 15th.

<u>Nine Saint Gillian Street</u>

The house creaked and groaned as it settled into the night. The unfamiliar noises made Ben nervous. No sounds of the night creatures hunting for food, no owls flapping their wings and hooting above his head. No wind blowing the leaves in the trees. It was quiet, and still he couldn't sleep.

He had a cot in Rowanne's room, but he didn't sleep on it. He slept beside her on her bed. She was his mate, and he couldn't bear to be far away from her.

The room was pitch dark, but Ben had reflective vision at night. His eyes glowed orangey-yellow, and he could see in the dark. His skills were honed from years of living in the forest. Sometimes he hunted at night as well as in the daytime if he needed food.

Ben lay still beside Rowanne, not wanting to wake her. She was tired from talking to the policewomen about the bad men who took her. She didn't want to talk about them or think about them anymore.

Ben didn't know the bad men. He'd never seen them, but he'd heard them when they came to take Rowanne.

That was enough to make him hate them with a passion.

With hearing as sharp as any fox, Ben heard a click downstairs at the front door. He sat up, listened for a moment, and then he heard a footstep on the stairs.

Ben slipped out of bed without disturbing Rowanne. Softly he padded to the door and stepped out into the dark hallway. He closed Rowanne's door behind him, crouched down against the wall, and waited. He smelled their scents and recognized them from the forest.

As the danger came closer to Rowanne's door, Ben felt the sensation surge through his body, and he lost control of his temporary humanity. He shifted.

With a little yip he sprang off the floor and clamped his jaws around the throat of the bad man. Tasting human flesh and blood did not please him, but he'd tasted worse. He had to protect Rowanne from these men. Men who would take her away from him and sell her for money.

Growling and ripping flesh like he'd done hundreds of times in the forest, Ben tore the first man apart, left him bleeding outside Rowanne's door, and ran down the stairs on all fours after the second bad man.

The man had come halfway up the stairs, caught a glimpse of what Ben was doing to his friend and turned and retreated.

As he was running away, Ben sped up and caught him before he reached the front door. He jumped on the man's back and knocked him down the same way he'd knocked down small deer in the forest when he was starving.

As the man struggled and tried desperately to get

away, Ben used his razor-sharp teeth and tore the man's throat out.

Covered in blood, the animal part of Ben propelled him outside and down the front walk. His animal instinct was to run.

Ben ran and kept on running.

Luke woke thinking he heard a noise in the hallway—a growling noise followed by a thump. Hoodoo was his first thought. The big Bernese Mountain dog was always bouncing around and knocking things over with his bulk.

Padding into the hall to check out the disturbance, Luke sucked in a breath when he flicked on the light. Roland Rancourt, at least Luke thought it used to be Roland Rancourt, lay mutilated and covered in blood outside Rowanne's bedroom door.

Ben.

"Ben, where are you, Ben?" Luke called in a whisper. He ran back into his room as quietly as he could and pulled on a pair of jeans and a t-shirt. Once he dressed, Luke ran downstairs to see how Rancourt had gained access to the house.

There was no way he should have been able to get in without sounding the alarm.

At the bottom of the stairs lay another corpse, torn apart by razor-sharp animal teeth precisely like the one upstairs.

Ben.

The front door stood wide open, and Luke took it as

a sign Ben was gone. He walked outside, glanced up at the moon, and wondered how he'd explain the condition of the two dead men to the police.

He couldn't. No dog would have killed two humans and left them in such a state. Possibly a crazed Pit Bull, but he'd have to invent a Pit Bull, and he wasn't a very good liar.

Luke ducked back inside, closed the front door, and locked it behind him. He stepped over the carnage splattered across the marble floor in the foyer and hurried upstairs to ask Misty what they should do.

"What's happening, sweetheart?" Misty was sitting on the side of the bed. "I heard you get up. Did you go downstairs?"

"Yes, I did. We have a problem, sweetheart, and we need a quick solution if you can think of one."

Misty shrugged on her fuzzy pink robe and followed Luke into the hallway to view the damage. "Oh, my goodness. Ben is an efficient killer, isn't he?"

"He ran, Mist. I don't know where he is."

"Let's worry about finding Ben later. First we have to put this guy somewhere where it will look completely natural for him to be torn apart like he is."

Luke tried not to smile but failed miserably. The guileless way Misty expressed herself always made him laugh. "This was the man who took Rowanne and sold her like a piece of meat to his friends."

"Then he got what was coming to him, didn't he? Let me think. How about a quick trip to the bayou, and we'll let the gators have at it."

Luke nodded. "That's a plausible solution. I'll get Casey to help me get them to the truck."

"Remove their wallets," said Misty, "as a precaution. Just a suggestion. You're the police officer."

"A good suggestion," said Luke. "You're always level headed, my beloved one."

"Thank you for that, though we both know that's not true. Eww, you need plastic. I don't want blood in my new truck."

"Copy that," said Luke. He ran down the hall and opened the door of Casey's room. "Wake up, Casey. We've got a situation." Both the dogs jumped up from the mat beside Casey's bed. Sleeping in Casey's room with the door closed, they hadn't heard the intruders.

"What kind of situation, Luke?" Casey sounded groggy.

"The dead bodies kind. I need help, right away."

"I'll get dressed." Casey sat on the side of the bed in his boxers. "What time is it?"

"Four in the morning."

"Shit."

"Ditto."

A couple of minutes later, Casey shuffled out of his room, fully clothed, and focused on the corpse in the hallway. "What in seven hells happened to him?"

Luke dropped the plastic tarp and shrugged. "The same thing that happened to the guy at the bottom of the stairs—Ben."

Casey's dark eyes widened. "Ben did this? How is that possible? This guy looks like... don't know."

"Ben was protecting Rowanne."

"Two of them? Are these the men after Row?"

"That's my guess. See if you can find the wallet, ID, and cell phone of the guy downstairs, then come back and help me roll them in the tarps."

Casey gazed at the bloody mess at his feet and nodded. "Sure, Luke. I'm on it."

"Hang on. I'll get you a pair of latex gloves."

"Good thought. Where are we taking them?"

"Gator country."

"Yep, good one. How did they get so... mangled?"

"Ben."

"He did this with his bare hands?"

"Nope. With his teeth and claws. Ben is a shifter, and when he's threatened he becomes a fox."

Casey shook his head. "No way. That's soooo cool. It also explains a lot."

Luke left the dogs in Casey's room to keep them away from the blood and the gore. He and Casey rolled up Rancourt, and his buddy and duct-taped them inside the plastic. They lugged them out to the truck, tossed them into the back of the Ford Expedition and closed the hatch.

Misty followed them outside. "Take them to Gran's and dump them in the swamp. I'll do cleanup while y'all are gone."

Casey made a face. "You have the worst job, Mist. That is one horrible mess in there."

"I'll work my Molly Maid magick."

South of Houma

An hour later, Luke backed the Expedition into Gran's driveway and shut off the engine. The little bungalow was all in darkness. "I'm glad she has no close neighbors."

Casey chuckled. "Me too. Although I *am* with a cop if we happen to get caught."

"Don't remind me. I think there's enough moonlight we can see the way to the river." He opened the hatch, tugged on the tarps, and rolled the two bodies out onto the ground.

"How do you want to do this?" asked Casey.

"Roll them to the edge of the water, and we'll unwrap them there."

"Yep."

The slow-moving bayou passed only a few dozen feet behind Gran's old bungalow. Where she was situated, high on the bank, she'd never been bothered by flooding.

One at a time, they rolled the bodies out of the tarps and pushed them over the berm of mud into the water. One small splash each, but it was enough of a disturbance to alert the gators watching with glowing yellow eyes and listening for sounds of their next meal.

The blood would draw them too.

Wild thrashing, splashing, and gnashing of teeth

came next. The crunching of bone was unsettling behind them as Luke and Casey rolled up the two bloody tarps into huge wads of disgusting sticky plastic.

"What are we going to do with these?" asked Casey.

"There's an industrial incinerator in Houma," said Luke. "I knew the gate code. As long as they haven't changed it, we'll toss them in there."

Casey nodded as he closed the hatch on the stinking tarps.

Familiar with Houma, the place he grew up and attended high school, Luke drove through the industrial park, punched in the code, and breathed a sigh of relief as the gate unlatched. He drove to the parking lot behind one of the incinerators and stopped long enough to toss the tarps in.

"I'll have to get Misty's truck detailed as soon as I can get an appointment," he said. "The blood smell will linger even if I spray it."

As they drove home to New Orleans, Casey asked, "Where do you think Ben would run off too? He doesn't know anything about the city."

"No idea. We'll have to search for him in the morning. Rowanne won't be happy that he's gone."

"That's for damn sure," said Casey. "She's an entirely different person since she met him."

"She learned a lot about life in a few days. She hasn't said much, but she's been through a traumatic experience. I'm sure more happened to her than what she told the detectives."

Casey nodded. "She's handling it well. I give her points for maturity that I never knew she had."

"Row was always a sweet kid before she hit puberty," said Luke. "Then she lost her mother. She's had a lot to deal within a short time."

Nine Saint Gillian Street

Rowanne woke at first light, and Ben wasn't in her room. She tore into the bathroom, and he wasn't there either.

Maybe he was hungry and went downstairs. He's always hungry.

She got dressed and hurried down to the kitchen. Misty and Luke were drinking coffee and looking oddly worried. "What's wrong? Something happened to Ben, didn't it?"

Luke pointed to the seat opposite him and nodded. "Sit down, Rowanne, and I'll tell you."

Rowanne tears started before she even started across the floor. She never cried. "Don't take Ben away from me. Don't. I'll die if you do."

"We didn't take him away, Row, he left." Luke reached for her hand, and she jerked it away. "Listen to me. Okay? Calm down and listen to what I'm saying."

"He wouldn't just leave," she sobbed.

"The men who took you came last night while you were sleeping. They broke into the house and Ben heard them. He got out of bed, and he killed them."

Panic brought another round of sobbing. "Did they hurt him? Is that what you're not telling me?"

Luke raised his hand. "Rowanne, enough. Listen to me. Are you listening?"

She inhaled a couple of breaths, stopped crying, and sat quietly. "Okay, I'm listening."

"Ben shifted when danger was coming for you. He killed the men and then ran away."

"We're going to go out and look for him," said Misty. "We were waiting for you to get up so you could come with us."

"Okay. I get it. When he shifts back, he'll want to come back to me."

Misty nodded. "That's right, but he doesn't know the city, and he might be lost."

Rowanne nodded. She sat quietly and inhaled a few deep breaths. "I'm okay now. What did you do with the dead guys? Was one of them the boss I identified for the cops?"

Luke nodded. "We got rid of the bodies, and we're not going to talk about them. Okay?"

Rowanne made a face. "Y'all didn't call the police so… I don't get it. Why not? You're a cop, Uncle Luke. What did Ben do to them?"

"Let's just say the way Ben left the two men was not something we could explain to the police. He attacked them as a fox. We had to dispose of them another way. I'd rather not recall the details before breakfast."

"Okay. I don't want Ben getting into trouble for something he couldn't help doing. He always tries to protect me."

"Yes, he does," said Luke. "And he did one hell of a job."

After breakfast, Casey, Rowanne, Luke, and Misty piled into the Expedition and began searching the city for Ben. They covered city parks, open green spaces and parkland on both sides of the Mississippi for miles and miles. There was no sign of him.

Rowanne's eyes were red-rimmed from crying the whole time they were searching. "Do you think he'd get as far as his forest?"

"That's at least twenty-five miles north of the city," said Luke. "Could he run that far in a short time?"

"Maybe he's not there yet, but on his way," said Misty. "We could be waiting for him when he gets there."

Rowanne began sobbing again. "What if he's scared of the city now and wants to go back and live in the forest?"

"I think you'll have to talk to him, sweetheart, to find out."

Rowanne nodded and swiped at her eyes with her shirt sleeve. "Right. I need to talk to him."

Luke drove out to the highway and began driving north. His cell rang on his belt, and Detective Scarlett's number came up on the screen.

"Detective Scarlett, you have news for me?"

"I wanted to thank you for putting us on to the estate on the golf course, Ranger Hyslop. We found a mountain of evidence there against Rancourt, and several other prominent businessmen. Fingerprints of four young gangers with records came up in the system, and we've issued warrants for their arrests."

"Glad to help," said Luke.

"One other thing," said Scarlett, "Lieutenant White came into my office to apprise me of a development this morning."

"Oh, what kind of development?"

"Roland Rancourt's wife arrived at the precinct and filed a missing person's report on her husband."

"Rancourt is missing?"

"His wife seems to think so."

"If she knew the truth, she might not want him back."

"True enough," said Scarlett. "I know I wouldn't want him back. You have a nice day, Ranger Hyslop."

Luke drove on thinking about the bone-crunching sound the gators made the night before in the bayou. Roland Rancourt wouldn't be returning to his wife.

The sound of Rowanne's voice behind him snapped him out of the unpleasant memory.

"Which way would Ben come to the forest, Uncle Luke?"

"The quickest way from New Orleans is to come from the south end. Shall we see if we can access the south side?"

"Yes, please."

Luke hadn't driven around the park, like Misty had. "Did you drive on the south side of the forest, sweetheart?"

"No. When I came to pick y'all up, I drove from the golf course up and around the other way."

"So, we've covered all the roads around the forest except for the south side. We'll have to find our way." Luke fiddled with the GPS and brought up a map on the screen.

"There, I see it," said Misty. "A dirt road running along the south side." She programmed the south side of the state forest into the navigation system and hoped for the best.

Without an exact address, it was iffy.

The system guided them to the road, and Luke turned right. "We should be driving right across the bottom of the park. Keep your eyes open for Ben."

"I'm watching," said Casey. "All I see are trees."

For hours they drove around the perimeter watching for any sign of Ben—the boy, or Ben—the fox and saw neither one.

"It's almost dark," said Luke. "We have to give it up for today and go home."

"No," cried Rowanne. "I want to get out and walk. He'll smell me and come find me."

"No, Rowanne," Luke said firmly. "That's not happening tonight. We were unprepared last time, and I learned my lesson. If we're going to tramp to the hunting shack, we'll do it in the morning, and we will be a lot more prepared this time."

"All right," said Rowanne. "I should get some things

of Ben's together anyway before we start searching."

"Thank you for being reasonable, Row," said Luke.

"You're welcome, Uncle Luke. Thanks for everything you've done for Ben and for me. I owe you and Misty a lot."

"You're welcome, sweetheart."

CHAPTER SIXTEEN

Thursday, February 16th.

<u>Nine Saint Gillian Street</u>

Rowanne was up at dawn's first light, searching her room for everything she needed to take with her in case she didn't come back. She packed up the clothes Misty had bought for Ben, his arrow he used for a wand, and the poppet he'd made her for Valentine's Day.

Before putting her boots on, she put some of Misty's healing salve on her blisters and covered her heels with Band-Aids. She slipped on a pair of socks and eased her feet into her army boots.

Rowanne carried her heavy pack downstairs and joined Misty, Luke, and Casey in the kitchen for a quick breakfast before they left.

"I want to take Nixa," said Rowanne. "Ben will want her if he's staying in the forest and not coming back."

Misty nodded. "Yes, that's a good idea."

Luke and Casey had amassed bottled water, flashlights, matches, sleeping bags, blankets, and food— at least enough for a couple of days.

"I'm taking a Garmin this time," said Luke. "It's so

easy to get turned around in the forest and go in the wrong direction."

"My phone is charged," said Casey. "It will work this time if there's service."

"Please be careful." Misty walked to the back gate as they packed the Expedition. "You might not be able to call me if you lose phone service again."

"I'll watch it carefully," said Luke. He kissed her goodbye, and his gaze narrowed on her. "You're pale today, sweetheart. Please take a day off and rest."

"I will rest today. Don't worry."

Louisiana Forest

When they neared the forest, Rowanne said, "I want to start behind the estate house and walk to the hunting shack. That's where Ben will be if he's all the way back from the city."

"Okay," said Luke. "I'll circle up that way first."

Luke drove farther north and turned on the golf club road. They passed the course, but there were no players. Too early in the season.

"Yellow tape on the front door of the house," said Casey as they passed by.

"No more wild parties there," said Rowanne with an icy edge to her voice.

Luke was sure more had happened to her than she'd shared with the detectives.

By looking at the map and guessing the location of

the cabin, he edged along another service road as far as they could go. If he had things right, he'd cut about six or seven hours of walking off the trip.

When they arrived at what he thought would be the closest spot to access the cabin, Luke parked the truck. He and Casey unloaded the hatch and hefted the heavy packs holding their supplies.

Rowanne shouldered her own backpack and carried a bag holding extras. "Come on, Nixa. Let's go find Ben."

After trudging along for two and a half hours, the terrain started to look familiar, and they made their way into the tiny clearing with the wooden shack.

Rowanne's face lit up when she saw the little place. Luke hoped Ben had come back there for her sake. She was counting so heavily on finding him there. A long way to run from the city, even for a fox, but he might have managed it by now.

The fire pit was hot as they passed it, and there was a scent of meat in the air. Luke had hope that Ben was back home.

Rowanne ran ahead and pushed the door of the shack open. Ben was lying on the bare springs of the cot, his mattress forgotten at Misty's house.

He jumped up with a little mewling sound and pulled Rowanne close to him. "I didn't think...I didn't know..."

Filled with emotion, she held him tight and said nothing.

Luke and Casey set down their heavy loads and inhaled a couple of deep breaths. "I'm glad you're safe, son. We searched for you in the city."

"I killed the bad men when they came for my mate. I made a terrible mess and thought you might be mad at me. I didn't know what to do, so I ran."

Luke shook his head. "You did what you had to do. We're not mad. You protected Rowanne, and you acted in her defense. You can come home with us, or you can stay here in the forest. It's your life and your choice. Nobody can tell you what's best for you."

"I want to be with Rowanne, but I belong in the forest. I can't live in the city."

Rowanne nodded her head. "I realized that too. You can't live in the city, and I don't expect you to change your life for me. I'm staying here with you."

Luke rolled his eyes and waited for the scene to play out.

Rowanne held Ben's hand. "I love you, Ben. I'm your mate, and we have to be together."

Okay, Luke had totally lost control of this situation. "What about your father, Rowanne? He will want you at home with him in Baton Rouge as soon as he's well."

"Ben and I will talk to him when he's well enough to meet us at the edge of the forest. I sent him a text last night when I made up my mind about what I had to do. He already knows."

"He does?" Luke was floored by that.

"It's the right thing for me, Uncle Luke, and it's the only thing for Ben. Like you just said, my life, my choice, right?"

Well, that bit of wisdom had just come back to bite him in the ass. "I honestly can't see this working, Row. You don't belong out here."

She shrugged. "I've never belonged anywhere, Uncle Luke. I understand now. That's because I don't belong in a place, I belong with a person—with Ben."

How do you explain to a sixteen-year-old that being love-struck wouldn't keep you fed and clothed and happy for a lifetime? You couldn't. They'd have to figure it out on their own. "Okay, we'll play it your way for now. When your father gets out of the hospital in a few days, we'll be back, and we'll talk more then."

"I won't change my mind," Rowanne said.

Stubborn redhead. Luke hugged them both, then nodded towards the packs of supplies on the floor of the shack. "There are a few things in there y'all can use to make your lives a little more comfortable."

"Thanks," said Rowanne with a smile. "It will be nice to have a sleeping bag."

Ben and Rowanne stood hand-in-hand with Nixa beside them, watching Luke and Casey disappear into the trees. This was the right decision. For them, it was the only decision.

"I love you, Ben."

"I love you, red-haired girl."

~ THE END ~

Mom and I hope you're enjoying Misty's Magick & Mayhem as our cast of characters have their adventures.

When Misty was a recurring character in Mom's Blackmore series, so many readers saw that she was ready for a baby. It looked like it would be Blaine's but due to no fault or a lack of love between them, life took a different course. Mystere needs her beloved New Orleans to thrive. She needs her house and her father and everything that Nine Saint Gillian gives her. And now, it gave her Luke—another great love.

We love to hear your thoughts. Giving books a star rating and/or a review on Amazon means so much. It not only helps the authors, but also other readers find something new to read.

Mistys Magick & Mayhem
School for Reluctant Witches
School for Saucy Sorceresses
School for Unwitting Wiccans
Nine Saint Gillian Street
The Ghost of Pirate's Alley
Jinxing Jackson Square
Flame

As always, we love to hear from our readers. You can find us both Auburn Tempest and Carolina Mac on Facebook and Amazon.

Blessed Be

CPSIA information can be obtained
at www.ICGtesting.com
Printed in the USA
LVHW102204051222
734655LV00024B/645